# THE
# MADDING
# OF
# ELI McNAMARA

*'The greed of the living is naught
compared to the greed of the dead'.*

# JOHN F. WAKE

*'THE DESIRES OF THE DEAD HAVE SHADOWS'*

# THE MADDING OF ELI McNAMARA

Published in the United Kingdom by Pwntan
info@wales-tours.com
First Edition: September 2021.
Category: History / Crime, Social

## FOREWARD

Victorian seances led to extraordinary tales of spaces between heaven and hell. Within those spaces were trapped the dead on their final journey. Victorian mediums could control the living, but the dead were a different matter. This book is based on several facts and legends. The intertwining of the characters is loosely aligned on previously untold stories. The speculated locations of lost treasure may still be there. It is seen through the eyes of one Elijah Llewellyn McNamara who was brought up in the Royal public house, demolished now. Eli Llewellyn McNamara is a fictitious name and does not reference anyone by name, either dead or alive.

*The original family on which the McNamara's are based.*
*(Pic Copyright – Author)*

## PROLOGUE

I have given numbers to each piece of narrative, as if chapters in a book. The numbers signify each time I have added to my story to keep it in sequential order. There are often many months between sections as my mood and circumstances permit.

**My life is in ruins.** How could I have come to this? My early childhood was special. I wish I knew then what I know now; that is the cry of many a person, but they have not ended up incarcerated after the most unearthly of encounters. This lonely existence is most probably for the rest of my life, yet I hope one day the truth will be known.

*(Elijah L. McNamara)*

## CHAPTER ONE

Elijah Llewellyn McNamara I am told is a powerfully strong name. For that I obviously thank my mother and father. Elijah from my mother's Christian avocation, Llewellyn from the country of my birth, Wales, and McNamara from my Dad's Irish parents. I believe I have a large family in Ireland, but I know little of them. Mam and Dad were publicans and kept licensed premises, which later in life made me rather intolerant of fools, especially intoxicated ones! It is the reason I can put this narrative in some sort of overt honesty which can be relied upon, or at least can be examined seriously.

I am going to tell the tale which in truth is stranger than any other I have ever heard others tell. I will tell you the full story as I remember it. I will not mention precise locations, but some may well recognise them and possibly evoke malevolence, leading to unforeseen circumstances. My humanity I feel is real but the world I relate is not, the story is told from my head and not from my heart.

The land of Britain is full of magical tales, wizards and hero's and I always read those stories with the proverbial pinch of salt. Too many people over the centuries have been witness to the same terrifying happening that has led to the position I now find myself in.

The Royal public house was my residence from 1889, the year I was born, until 1907. Its situation adjacent to the river, and among a burgeoning residential suburb, made it a profitable and busy house. It had three distinct levels of human habitation, the top floor had seven bedrooms for the use of our family, my mother, father, and siblings of which there were six. The first floor was our family nursery and four other bedrooms for guests, if my parents wanted relatives or friends to lodge with us, in truth that was rare. On that floor also was our nursery, which seems now, many years later, as the wrong place to be, since a large billiard room was adjacent. The sound of men cursing became familiar to me, as did the clink clack of the billiard balls. My mother attempted to keep many of the customers out of the room whilst we were playing, but it was not an easy job. She was hard though on 'swearing and cussing' as she called it, telling many an adult man off as if they were juveniles. On the ground floor there were bars for the consumption of our beers and sitting rooms for the family and staff. There were three cellars below ground and two kitchens for our staff to prepare our food. One cellar room I was not allowed to enter, it being always kept secure.

At an early age I saw various sorts of behaviour from a variety of kinds of people. I also saw social distinctions, as it seemed my mother and father were the upper class, not because we lived on the top floor, but because the permanent workers in the Royal were classified as servants. It is a classification which seemed to go unnoticed by anyone, as everyone appeared to know their relative places. The only time I could officially enjoy the company of the 'servants' was on a Sunday when my mother and father dined in a basement kitchen. It was my mother's duty to prepare the meats, the servant's duties to prepare the vegetables and my father's duty simply to carve the meat. We all sat around a large table, the family and five staff. All was affable but always regimented. The pub was closed on a Sunday but after lunch the staff washed up and made ready for church, but my father served a few favoured friends in a room behind the bar, they having to knock three times to gain entry. I did not understand how no money passed hands, my father appearing to give the beer gratis. I found out later that he chalked the credits of the men (and it was all men) on small individual slates.

My father seemed to have a special acquaintance on those Sunday afternoons, a man who perhaps came once a month, a man who my father knew well. It all seemed so secretive. I was not introduced to the man and his friend, nor I think was my mother, she being fully engrossed in raising the family and running the pub. Her kindly ways were lost in the hubbub of daily pub life. She was indeed an efficient and very well-respected woman.

Schooling was difficult to fit into daily pub routines, yet my school in Wood Street was barely a few hundred yards away from the Royal. I seemed to be a popular student, apparently because I lived in a public house. Most of my fellow scholars lived in the terraced conurbation off Wood Street where there were no pubs and drinking of beer, I was told it was prohibited. If it was illegal and temperance was the directive, then nearly everyone was breaking the law! The sight of men, and women, carrying pitchers of ale then disappearing into their homes was an oft one. Seemed so odd to me as I lived in a public house where the consumption of ale and spirits were promoted, yet people living in those small, terraced streets, only a few hundred yards away from the

Royal, on the other side of the river, were ordered to abstinence. It was indeed a strange town.

Life went on, our large family living a reasonably comfortable existence in comparison to many of my school pals. Tom the drayman and my father were close friends. I had seen him scores of times call at the pub delivering barrels, and now Dad said it was my turn to climb up onto the dray to deliver beer to a public house several miles away. Tom had agreed. It was a day I had dreamed about and now it had arrived. I must have been around ten or eleven years of age. He picked me up at ten one morning stating he would be back to the Royal around five, Tom having to go only a little further to the brewery to unload and see to the horses. This short route took him past those streets dedicated by the 'powers that be' to temperance. Occasionally he would come into the Royal for a pint as he was a fine drinking man. Tom had two magnificent shire horses which he loved dearly, named Moses and Abraham, which were part of the stabling near to the brew house. It seemed all draymen were loyal to their various equine friends, only sharing their horses when one was unwell.

That long day sat high upon the dray next to Tom is a golden memory of my life. The gritting sounds of the wheels, the proud heads of the horses flinging up and down, the haulage up the hills where I felt great sympathy for those enormous beasts. In one of our endless conversations, I told him of my most recent dream where I was running away from a lion. Tom stood up and pulling back the reins he brought the dray to a halt. In his loudest of voices, he stated, 'Dreams are toys', another pull on the reins and a shout of 'on' and the dray started up again. When I enquired of him what he meant he stated that William Shakespeare thought that dreams are just toys for the mind to play with whilst in sleep. That was the power of Tom to impress. 'What do you know of ghosts young Eli?' This was a strange question as he knew I knew nothing. I looked at him and he at me, expecting an answer which did not come. 'By the pricking of my thumbs, something wicked this way comes' he said, then he looked directly into my face. For a moment I was scared, but his face turned into a huge grin as he lifted the whip and cracked it in the air over the horses. 'Shakespeare' he boomed, 'He knew about ghosts and apparitions'. The laugh then seemed to inspire the shires with new energy and the dray increased in speed. The days with Tom on the dray delivering the barrels, were days when I had not a care in the world and my life was halcyon and special.

Tom always called in at a small cottage adjacent to the main lane not far from our destination. My duty was to stay with the dray, 'for security and friendship to the horses' he would say. He was met at the door by a man who would wave at me before they would both disappear within. This man always wore a pale blue shirt with no collar, black trousers, highly buffed boots and light canvas bracers. His demeanour and stance were very impressive, and he seemed known to me. On one occasion he came to the horses and stroked them, gave me a wink, before disappearing back inside the cottage. I recognised him as one of my father's Sunday afternoon acquaintances in the Royal. It was this man I had also seen coming up from the cellar with my father. Tom and the man would be inside the cottage for many minutes, sometimes approaching I am sure half an hour. I remember once Tom returning to climb up on the dray next to me, and as we both waved goodbye to the man, he shouted, 'The sands are numbered that make up my life. Here must I stay, and here my life must end'.

I found those words quite frightening as they had no context in any conversations prior. He went inside slamming the door behind him. Tom pulled hard on the reins and said, 'On my beauties, on, on'. Moses and Abraham reacted in perfect harmony then the dray, the barrels, Tom and I slowly made our way back home.

I said to Tom, 'Were they Shakespeare's words too?' He answered with a smile so broad that the answer must have been 'yes'.

The way of the lane was full of treasures, blackberries, willowherbs, periwinkles, thrushes, dunnocks, all and much more pointed out by Tom to his eager student. There was no evil in my life, no modicum of thought of such. Everything was idyllic, so was the innocence of childhood.

The last time I ever travelled with Tom, he told me that his duty was at an end. He had told my mother not to pack cheese and pickle as he was arranging a lunch stop and it was his treat. That lunch stop was to make a great impression on me. At ten I was ready to depart as soon as Tom called at the Royal. Bertha, the pub cook, gave me a kiss and apologised for not packing me a lunch. She made me promise to inform Tom that he could call at any time to her kitchen for a beer and cheese if he was passing. I felt that Bertha had a soft spot for Tom, as it appeared most of the servants did, they being mostly women. The only man downstairs was our cellarman who hardly spoke and was not a person to get close to. 'Efficient, grumpy but useful', my father used to describe him.

We made our way from the Royal, across the moorland, and within the usual time we arrived outside the cottage. All was serene. The country flowers were on show everywhere, but I could not name them, nor I doubt could any boy of my age. I did know roses of course, and they were the overriding occupants of the cottage garden.

Tom rose, stood, and offered me his arm saying, 'That which I would discover the law of friendship bids me to conceal'. He climbed down and beckoned me to stand down also. 'Yes, that was Shakespeare. You're coming with me to meet someone'. He walked down the flag stoned way to the cottage, and as he did, the door opened and there was the man. He was buttoning up his tunic and I saw that he was a policeman. I will admit I was shocked not thinking one moment that a man of the law lived so deep in the country and away from any troublemakers. The constables I have known were fearsome and kept law and order, even within the public bars when necessary, in a most ferocious way. I dreaded them. This man smiled and on entering the cottage I saw a veritable feast laid out on the table.

Tom spoke, 'This is Constable Jeremiah Williams. he is my best friend and as you are a best friend too, I thought we all ought to meet'. I looked around the room. Neat, predominant colour dark red, two armchairs, mantelpiece with wooden framed mirror sat on it. The curtains were long to the floor and red in colour. A huge black saucepan sat on the fire and bubbled away. It was from this saucepan Constable Williams scooped water to put in a white, plain teapot which he covered with a cosy, having a woollen bird as a handle. The small room exuded a kind of wellbeing, and I could imagine the officer sitting in his armchair, with his feet up on the mantlepiece enjoying an ale after his duty. I noticed that there were many books on a single shelf that stretched the whole length of one wall in the room. I expected them for some reason, to be all relative to Shakespeare's dramas, but they were not. They had strange names, several of which contained words in the titles relating to apparitions, demons, ghosts. I saw that both men were looking straight at me and had noticed my interest towards the bookshelf.

Jeremiah Williams smiled and beckoned me to sit down. 'Well son you are honoured', said Tom as he sat at the table. 'Jeremiah has set you a place so sit down and start eating, you are our guest'. I did exactly as I was told and filled my blue patterned plate with cheese, chives, bread and pickle to which I tucked in. I felt special and very grown up. I was a tall boy and of a good stature, but Jeremiah was enormous, a man I was in awe of as soon as I set my eyes on him.

I was told by my host, that he, Tom and my father had regular meetings in various places in the town centre. I know my mother never attended such meetings, she always working behind the bars and running our pub. They informed me they had formed a Shakespeare Society of which they were the only three members which rather naively in those early years, I believed.

Once the fare was finished it was time to go.

'Listen young Eli' said Jeremiah, 'Remember these words. Like father, like son. Proverbs are never wrong. Always remember that. Your father is a wonderful man'.

A man of Jeremiah's countenance ensured those words would not be forgotten. If I was going to be like my father I was pleased. How can words mean so much to me? Tom took me by the arm and led me to the door, turning and wishing Jeremiah farewell we left the cottage and climbed up on the dray. I asked Tom why Jeremiah had told me that. He kind of brushed my question away with loud commands to the horses who took on their duties immediately in the most disciplined of fashion. His only comment was, 'Jeremiah is being Jeremiah. A man of words.'

After the delivery, and hours later, we slowly 'clip-clopped' our way back in the direction of my town. Tom stopped the dray once more outside Jeremiah's cottage, this he had never done before on the way home. 'I have forgotten something that we have for you. Stay there'. He climbed down and entered the cottage without knocking on the door returning almost immediately. 'Here, this is for you'. He handed me a book, the title of which read, History of the Kings of Britain. 'You will enjoy the read young Eli. Take great notice of Geoffrey the writer. Now come on, we're going home'. I said nothing. I could not understand why I would want to read a royal history of Britain. The only other mention of the volume was just before I waved goodbye to Tom outside the Royal.

'Read between the lines Eli. In many ways it is more important than the book itself'. I watched the dray cart make its slow and noisy way back to the brew house.

## CHAPTER TWO

The months passed. I was not a happy person, as all around me there seemed to be change. My parents were not happy, I could see that, their smiles were forced, and Dad always seemed to be in another place in his thinking. My mysterious cellar room was no longer a secret, as it was now being left unlocked. I went inside a few times and saw that it just contained a table and four chairs. There were candle remnants and not much else. It seemed its usefulness was over. It was a cold room with heavy brick walls and of course, no windows. Even my lovely Bertha seemed to be affected by all the unpleasant feelings and actions of my parents, which was not good. I was experiencing little asides between them also, which on some occasions involved me. I remember trying to please them more than ever, nothing was too much trouble in attempts to appease and then assist them. My siblings did not get the freedom I did, being often locked in their rooms for no apparent reason.

When I reached the age of thirteen years, the most unreal of news was imparted to me by father. I was in the snug of the Royal at the time and father was with Tom. I was to leave and attend a school in Somerset, near a town called Weston-Super-Mare. It was a blow as if a hammer had struck me squarely on the head. I looked both at Tom and father disbelieving at the news, but Tom smiled and gently raised his head up and down in a positive manner. I remember asking how long it would take to get home every night. I was informed I was not to do so, the school was to be my home also. Tom smiled that smile of reassurance and nodded his head up and down slowly, he told me it would make a man of me. I left the snug and went to my bedroom where I sobbed for some time. My mother, who was strong but a very fair and measured lady, came to my room and explained that the Boer Wars could start all over again, and the world seemed an unstable place. It seemed she wanted me away as well. One sentence resonated with me, and I recall it now.

'Elijah, you are an intelligent boy, far above your years. Your progress is being held back in Wood Street school. Soon you will leave and make your way in life. We have chosen you from the family to make good, and with extra schooling, perhaps you can support your less gifted siblings once we are gone'.

I had deep and uncorroborated feelings that my father wanted me away from the Royal, my mother also.

My siblings had been instructed to work and make a life of their own. Is that what a good family life should be? Distribute your children about the country among friends and relatives and let them fend for themselves? I was deeply disturbed and in truth I did not want to go. A new school at my age, a new country, and a new life. None of my friends would have to endure such. I informed my parents, in no uncertain terms, that I simply did not want to go. A few days of arguments were to no avail. I found myself two weeks later being conveyed by horse and trap to the dockside and put onto a steamer to take me to Weston-Super-Mare. The substance of my boat trip is not one of any worth to this story, other than to say I was put into the care of the Purser who deposited me on a beach pier some one hour later. From there I was picked up by another horse and trap and conveyed to school. I was well and truly out of the way of my Dad and Mam. My only real memory of the boat trip, other than apprehension, was the steam reciprocating engines that drove the paddles, the power transfixed me for virtually the whole journey.

The imposing, yet dreaded school is a separate story, but I did well, I swam in competitions, I achieved in classwork and enjoyed a night or two back home every six weeks or so. I had communicated by letter to my father, something I did often in the first few weeks, but decidedly less as the months passed. Each time my father met me at the Pier Head conveying me, sometimes by tramcar, other times by cab home to the Royal. I was noticing an even greater change between my father and mother, their relationship seemed strained. Whereas once they laughed together, held each other's hands and enjoyed family wit, they now hardly spoke. They undertook their relative jobs with the usual gusto, but not together, it seemed they were growing apart. Furthermore, my father looked pale and gaunt as though he was not eating, yet I saw him often devouring large amounts of the servant's fare.

I overheard my mother cursing at my father, calling him stupid. Why, I did not know, and was vexed by it all. There seemed less interest in me and my scholarly or sporting achievements.

My final day at Boarding School coincided with great celebrations in my hometown, which luckily, I was to experience. I was now sixteen years of age and waved a flag, along with thousands of others, at the procession and the bands. It meant nothing to me, I suppose I was lost in the fun, but looking back it was an important event, the day my town became a city. I remember little else other than our pub was packed with people and the drinking seemed to last for days. From my upstairs bedroom I could hear singing, shouting and the smoke from pipes and cigarettes seemed to permeate every corner of the house. Dad and Mam were working, it seemed, harder than ever before. I could not fault them for that, but I did not like the hostility, I felt loathing, one to the other. He seemed in another place, his mind not on his job. The more mistakes he made the deeper the rift that was opening between them.

I often cogitated on the worth of my schooling in Somerset. One thing for sure was it had taught me how to handle myself, I had boxed and represented the school at swimming. My grasp of life was extensive as I had mixed with boys from varying backgrounds, mostly rich, and their life skills initially brought me to feel third class. Some became friends and I realised that our upbringings make us what we are. None of us, I felt, should attempt to force our way of life and knowledge into the minds of others, with differing upbringings. We are what we are. I was sure though that my political, historical, and geographical knowledge was vast compared to my erstwhile Wood Street school friends. I was now a tall man and big, over six feet and heavily built. This gave me an appearance of many years older than I was. In my room I had hung boxing gloves, the ones I wore when I became the school heavyweight boxing champion. In the next few years I grew up quickly, noting how to handle drunkards, aggression, misplaced sentiment and the assorted personalities that seemed to congregate within and without of the Royal.

There was one character though who affected my life, both then and in later years, like no other, Tom! His honesty, his kind demeanour, his manner and his lifestyle made me look up to him as a kind of saint but in truth he was, as my father told me, a forthright member of the working classes. Please do not think my father above his station, he was not, but it was the way it was. Tom lived not far away in Scott Street. His rugged moustachioed face, bellowing laugh, odd clothing and bodily strength was addictive to all he met, especially the ladies to whom he winked constantly much to the annoyance of husbands and sweethearts. In those early years of my adulthood I was bewitched by Tom. The relationship between my father and Tom was a strange one. I saw how they would disappear into a corner and talk. These conversations sometimes lasted many minutes, being usually broken up by my mother whose patience was minimal. If she knew what they were deep in conversation about she certainly did not say, but she did not approve, that was for sure.

# CHAPTER THREE

My father had enrolled me in the St Mary Street brewery which had recently been taken over by two brothers, an associate of one of the brothers was a regular caller to the Royal. My job was to learn the beer trade from top to bottom, it was he who surely had secured my employment. My examination results from the Weston-Super-Mare school were excellent and indeed helped in securing this apprenticeship. I was one of several apprenticed to the brewery but felt perhaps overconfident as my upbringing had been in the brewery trade and my size an advantage. In more ways than one, people looked up to me. One day I returned home to the Royal and my mother found me as soon as I entered the pub. She looked concerned. 'Eli, I'm glad you're home. You will have to work this evening. Your father is unwell'.

I gave her a hug and said, 'Of course Mam I will. What's wrong with Dad?'

'He will not go to the doctor which we all want of course, including the staff. He has lost weight and is drawn. I'm worried about him'.

Her concern pleased me. Perhaps it was the concern for a fellow human rather for a husband by his wife. This was tempered with the thoughts for Dad's health. She turned away and returned to the public bar area and I went to my room. Over the next few weeks my father levelled out. His refusal to seek medical assistance, he claimed, helped his recovery, something I just could not understand. He had changed. His weight, his personality, his whole being was different, but that did not stop him from working. He looked ill but did not act it. My father, with a reason at the time not known to me, took work on ships departing the great Bute Docks. My mother did not seem to mind and coped very well with the domestic and day to day running of the pub. It appeared she thought that the sea air and travel may do him good. My father's days away initially were not many, usually leaving on a Thursday or Friday and returning four or five days later. Those periods of working away were to increase.

One evening Tom came to the pub and asked to speak to me. My father was home and took Tom and I to the gentlemen's snug, which at the time was empty, and stayed with us whilst Tom imparted the following knowledge. 'Jeremiah is leaving the constabulary'. He has informed his superiors that the employ does not suit his beliefs. He is a Christian man and wants to take up the cloth and for that reason he is going away for several weeks to England'. My father just nodded as though he was already aware of Jeremiah's decision. I did not understand why I was being informed.

'Eli, come here', said my father. I did so and stood next to him. 'You are now twenty years of age, a strong lad with a pleasing character. Your career is sound, and I am proud of you. You are also incredibly fit, and you run like the wind. I have seen you. Your athleticism makes me wish I were young again. Jeremiah, Tom, and I have a duty for you to perform and with that duty we must have trust. It will be between the four of us'. I stared at my father not knowing what was coming next. He could obviously see a look of curiosity on my face which was hardly helped by his next comment. 'You are not to tell your mother anything, she is a busy lady running this pub and whatever we do or say is between us, and us alone. Do you understand?' I nodded in a positive manner. At that point Bertha, the cook, came into the snug quite unannounced and enquired whether we all, especially Tom, wanted some refreshments. She was followed in by my mother who politely 'shooed' Bertha away. The meeting then regrettably came to an end and the men puffed on their pipes and chatted and anything secret was immediately forgotten.

Tom said quite casually, 'Eli, Jeremiah was asking if you had read the book he leant you, as he wants it back'. I had forgotten all about it. It was obvious though that Tom was simply changing the subject. I made my way to my room. I promised myself I would read it and return the volume as soon I had done so. I felt a little guilty that the book had lain there unread for a considerable time, in fact, years! It was all so odd and unreal, and I was a little uneasy with these strange happenings in my life.

Sleeping that night was not easy. Usually, I lay my head deep into the feathers, blocking out the raucous sounds of the pub percolating through the floorboards. I was not used to excitement at bedtime, it was an acceptance of routine which aided my slumber. I went over my father's words time and time again. Why were the three important men in my life wanting to trust me and not my mother? Sleep finally came at a late hour. The pub was quiet, and all family and staff were in their beds too. I had resided in the Royal for almost twenty years, and the time seemed ready for a change, nothing was the same. All my siblings had gone, the girls in service as kitchen maids and the boys up country working on farms. I was the baby and wondered often whether that was ultimately my future, but at this time it certainly was not. I deemed myself lucky.

My mother and father hardly spoke. He came home from sea and paid monies into the household on a regular basis, but it was not a home anymore. The love was gone. I did not mention it, nor did Tom or my father, but I indeed wanted to know what they needed to impart to me. Their enthusiasm for the subject had gone also. I am a fast reader, but the History of the Kings of Britain slowed me down somewhat. Such a complex book and I had no idea why I was asked to read it. The author was a monk who lived and wrote in the 12th century. Old fashioned and in some ways a read within the realm of a fantasy. I had to go over some sentences time and time again to grasp their meaning. The writing was strong. I climbed inside the pages of the book. It was like no other book I have read before, as it painted a picture of a world I did not know, and of a time where our world was so different. I was not to know how the book was to affect me in the years to come. I remember once being asked by Tom, if I believed in ghosts, a question I did not answer. I remember looking up to the heaven's hoping that the Lord would not grant me an audience with such an apparition, just to appease my hero, Tom.

# CHAPTER FOUR

Two unforeseen and awful things happened to our family one Sunday morning in March 1910. I was 21 years of age. My mother unilaterally informed me that she was leaving the Royal as she could not cope any more. It was simply too big a pub to run on her own management as my father was hardly ever there, and when he was, he slept. I noted anger too. The servants, including Bertha, were to be dismissed with the proviso that they could be offered first chance at re-employment with the new Landlords. I was devastated. I had known no other home. She said she had been offered a much smaller public house to run with no servants and requiring only a few staff. Even though I was mature and strong I can remember weeping when I heard the news.

The very evening that Mam had told me about the move from the pub, another strange, and deeply upsetting, thing occurred. Tom ran in. His haste was halted by the sight of my mother behind the main bar. I was adjacent, assisting her to serve, yet really wanting to know more about the news she had given me earlier. Tom was with a young man I believed I knew. They were both breathless and agitated yet trying to be calm. I looked at my mother who seemed to be expecting bad news, and it was bad news she got. She signalled for me to follow her from the main bar area to the snug. Tom and the man came around and entered the space, which was conveniently empty, the time of day not being one where its use was needed.

'I think you should sit down Annie. I have some bad news'. My mother in the gentlest of ways refused and leant over the bar ready for whatever Tom had to say. I was standing next to her. The sounds of the pub could be heard, men arguing, and bar billiard skittles being knocked down with some hilarity and cheering.

'There has been an accident. I am afraid your Sidney, Eli's Dad, has left this world. He has passed away'. It was said as though within a normal conversation. It was as if Tom wanted to get it off his chest as fast as he could, and the very direct approach was the best. Tom and my mother stared at each other for what appeared many minutes, but in fact were seconds. The other man, who was around my age, bowed his head to the floor. I wanted to shout out that it was probably a mistake. Dad could not be dead. Instead, my silence was as noticeable as Mam's. The awful pause that followed seemed to wait for her to ask a question, which did not come.

She slowly dropped her forehead to her hands and after some seconds she looked towards Tom and said, 'Thank you.' I wanted to shout at the men, but Mam's state of grace made me hold back. The truth is I did not believe. My father dead, impossible!

Tom said, 'He was in an accident at sea, I have been told by Ron here, who works as an agent, that Sidney was working timber from Norway. Some cargo shifted and he was knocked overboard. An attached rope apparently caused his body to be dragged. The captain did all he could to help Sid, but the seas were rough, and the coast was near. They retrieved his body later. I am so sorry'. My mother called me to her, and we hugged. 'May I thank you for your time in coming to tell me the news. May I offer you refreshment?' Mother was an exceptionally brave woman and stoic in the extreme. This attribute I shared but could not help starting to sob. She stood and walked out and into the main bar once again. I guessed she was going to make sure the bars had staff and then seek somewhere quiet to cry. Even though Tom pushed me to do so, I refused to follow. I know my own mother and she would have wanted to be alone. I was deeply upset but found myself hiding my mood, as my mother had, to retain some form of dignity at a time of crisis.

The other man spoke. 'We were in Wood Street school together Eli. Remember me, Ron Scrivens?' It was a shock, but after a second or two I did indeed remember him. I put my hand forward to shake hands before I came around and sat with them in the snug. The next few minutes were taken up with remembrances of my father and his troubles of recent times. His state of health never recovered to what it used to be; his sallow complexion, mixed with his loss of weight, perhaps added to the reason as to why he had not been quick enough to get out of the way of the moving cargo. Ron and I shared some reminiscences of school days to be gently interrupted by my mother who returned carrying a tray. She placed it down on a table, pulled back the cloth and revealed large chunks of the staple white bread, pickles and cheese. In a jug I could smell and could see the steam rising, from a quantity of Bovril. She must have thought a beef drink was better than alcohol. In the circumstances of the news, she was probably right.

Tom did not leave until late that afternoon. He and my mother shared memories of Dad. I was left with Ron, which in truth I did not mind. He put his arm around my shoulder a few times when my eyes filled. This happened often as people were coming in to see us with condolences. Ron, if my memory had served me properly, was a much bigger lad. His stature in the class in school then, seemed to me much more than it was now. We had often been taken for brothers. He was also rather pale. It was indeed a harrowing time. The news had spread quickly, and the pub was becoming packed with people wanting to give their condolences and reminisce over my father. I thought at the time that my mother should have closed the Royal as a matter of respect, but she did not. I later thought that her wisdom in not doing so was exact. Loneliness at the hearing of bad news is sometimes counterproductive. Grief must be shared. In just one day I had been told of my father's death and my mother's proposed exit from the Royal. The events, both coming to light on the same day, was confusing for me.

I remembered Dad and the secret he wanted to

entrust, the secret that Tom, Jeremiah and Dad were carrying, and I was going to be trusted with. I had to know what that was.

The City Cemetery Main Gate

## CHAPTER FIVE

On the day of the funeral, the cortege left the Royal at 11am. There were important men from the brewery walking alongside the hearse, the four fine black horses, plumed and looking magnificent. I knew that the hiring of such a vehicle was expensive, but aware that mother had saved a great deal of monies in the bank during her thrifty working life. There was a horse and one carriage behind the hearse with four elegantly dressed gentlemen being carried thereon, Tom, Jeremiah, Ron and me. We had all paid an equal amount for the use of the carriage as an indicator as to how much we all thought of my father. The monies passed to my mother as a contribution to the expenses of the day.

I was so glad Ron was there, as a man of my age he was a blessing. I was still a little concerned at his countenance, he was becoming rather pallid. Numerous people followed the two carriages. Many were regulars at our pub, others were friends. I was deeply upset that my brothers and sisters did not attend their own father's funeral. I was later to find out that mother had not even written to them wanting them to stay away. Her reasoning was her own. The cortege arrived at the city cemetery where Sidney McNamara, my father, was laid to rest. I had never seen such an occasion and was moved yet finding the whole situation hard to believe. Afterwards the vicar from the Wood Street

Congregational Church had finished his awful duties, we all returned to the Royal. Bertha had prepared a magnificent table of what she described as 'bites'. I would suggest, or even say with some authority, that there was more beer drunk in the Royal that day than any other 'Wake' I had experienced. My mother called a halt to it at 10pm and the pub emptied. It was then my father's death hit me the hardest. I could not understand why and how he had died. The circumstance seemed straightforward, yet I believed differently. He had lost weight, he was of a pallid face, and his demeanour alien to any known to me before. He was always away, he was forever whispering in corners with man friends, which of course included Tom and Jeremiah.

I had heard of secret societies which met in large buildings away from curious eyes, but Dad's was here in the pub. There were so many unanswered questions and perhaps they should have stayed that way!

The next few weeks were difficult, and I was glad when the emotional turmoil died down. Dad's death though was the catalyst to a new understanding of his life and some shocking revelations. I only wish I had known his problems and conditions and felt quite hurt that he did not share them with me. After all I am a man now and responsive to serious concerns.

Mam was leaving the Royal in days to take over the Cottage public house and I found it emotive. It was going to be my home also, her world, let alone mine, had been turned upside down. Deep down inside I was hurting, the family and lifestyle I once knew, vanished for ever. It was as though he was gone, and now it was time for everyone to move on and forget him. I will never forget him; I miss him so much.

Tom arranged for me to attend a meeting in his house in Scott Street, about what, I was not privy too. It was though, something to look forward to, in fact I could not wait. Our move to another part of town went smoothly. Everyone only too willing to assist. My room was considerably smaller than at the Royal. In fact, the Cottage pub was tiny. It stood on the corner of two small, terraced streets in what seemed a concentrated residential area. There were two small bars, and most times one person behind the counter could serve both. The cavernous hotel we had just vacated seemed a palace in comparison.

I continued my apprenticeship with the brewery, who in fact supplied the beer to both establishments. It was not Tom any more with the dray deliveries. Times really had changed. My father's death was temporarily forgotten when I was attending my work at the brewery. The water bubbling up from the well underneath to make the beer was a salvation to me. I had no other thoughts other than the mysterious spring water and wondering where it came from.

Days passed and finally the evening came for my meeting with Tom. The distance was not far from my work to Scott Street. I made my way through much hustle and bustle, not only with local people, but travellers making their way down the streets to and from the railway station. One memory was of a 'Johnny Onion' man knocking the doors selling his wares. His bicycle, hung with scores of very large onions, was leaning against the wall of Tom's house. Everyone seemed to love 'Johnny Onion' yet no-one could speak his language. Present in the house was Jeremiah, Ron Scrivens and Tom. I was confused as to the reason for the meeting and what Ron Scrivens had to contribute.

After pleasantries and a large pot of tea, accompanied by bread and chitterlings, Tom stood. Jeremiah, Ron Scrivens and I, were sitting around a table in a small ground floor room. It was at the front of the tiny, terraced house which overlooked the street. The room, even though compact, contained a table, four chairs, a roll top desk, and an armchair. A huge aspidistra plant dominated the window ledge emanating from a shiny grass green china pot. Ron was looking ill. There could be no other description of him. Was it worry? His features were drawn, he had lost weight, yet he kept his smart appearance. Tom and Jeremiah were still of impressive countenance but not the men they were. Perhaps Dad's death had hit them all hard.

Tom spoke. 'Eli, you are the only one here who is unaware of what I am about to say'. He sat down as if he should not have stood up in the first place. To say I was curious would have been an underestimation and felt a little peeved as I was the only one there who had been deprived of any knowledge prior. 'We have kept this quiet as there are powerful city fathers who would relish the chance to ridicule us. Also, we do not want to spread alarm or fear amongst the residents of the city'. He paused to take a sip of tea. I was excited yet somehow apprehensive of the revelations that were to come. I remember thinking was this the curious belated meeting that had been talked about in the pub. 'Your father Eli was not ill before his untimely death, he was in a state of shock. His life was not his own'. I looked around the table at the other two and then back to Tom. The solemn looks on their faces indicated that worse was to come. There was a pause which seemed to last for ever but in truth was probably only a few seconds.

'Please come on, tell me about Dad', I demanded as I felt vulnerable in their company.

'Your father many months ago met Ron', said Tom finally getting around to talking. 'Ron was working, running for a shipping agent in Mountstuart Square. One morning he boarded your father's steamer to pass an invoice addressed to the captain, and whilst there got into a conversation with your Dad. As the conversation progressed Ron told your father that he had experienced a cruel visit from beyond the grave'. Tom ceased talking immediately as he must have seen a look of disbelief on my face. I looked towards Ron who nodded his head in support of Tom. 'Your father apparently laughed and ridiculed Ron in such a way that he upset him'.

'I was telling the truth. He did not want to believe it,' Ron had interrupted. 'Everyone had laughed but your father seemed to ridicule and told me to shut up and speak of it no more. When I saw him again a week or so later, he made a point of talking to me. His whole attitude had changed and questioned me on what I saw and where it was. I told him. His interest went so far as asking me to show him where it had occurred, and would I take him at the exact time and day the apparition had materialised'. Ron stopped his narrative when Jeremiah pulled him gently back into the chair.

Tom continued, 'Your father had shared the information with me, and I shared it with Jeremiah. The increased interest stemmed from a story that Jeremiah's grandfather had told him, with quite some force, of an apparition which appeared in the old Infirmary corridor the night before his wife died. Someone in the hospital told him that the apparition, of a lady in a grey dress, had been seen by several people and the sightings proceeded the demise of someone'.

'What's this to do with my father?' I snapped, 'He was a real Christian man. He did not believe in such fanciful claims.

During the silence that followed it came to me. Of course, they were not meeting for any Shakespeare stuff, they were meeting to discuss apparitions. They were looking for ghosts. And the book, what was that about? Within the conversation I noted that there were inconsistencies, it was a drama script being played out by poor actors.

Dad's loss of weight and complexion could well have been caused by an imagined visitation. It was a picture puzzle that was being pieced together bit by bit in the little room in Scott Street. It went quiet, which added to the sombre atmosphere. It was as though a death had occurred in our presence and we were deliberating over the newly deceased. I was angry that my father was being spoken of with some silliness. I kept remembering the proposed meeting to discuss something with me. It had never happened and perhaps if it had have done my father would be alive today. I wondered if my mother knew and therefore their relationship seemed to be more than tenuous in recent times. Jeremiah spoke,

'There is more to it Eli. Your father had been going to see a woman who had an office in the Waxworks. It is not far from here'. He paused as he could see me staring in disbelief. It was stupid and ridiculous, and I was thinking of walking out, but curiosity kept me there.

'He had become obsessed with a riddle, a riddle we have all become preoccupied with. Sid wanted information from certain dead people. He became sure one man could be contacted via mediums.

'He had been having headaches and was in trouble physically but kept on with seeing this one medium,

Madame Ella, as she called herself. She was telling him some strange things about the other side, seances, and about apparitions and ghosts. Your father seemed to be addicted to the subject. We have all become advocates of it. Eli, ghosts are a real phenomenon. I believe they torment humans and enjoy the control they have over them. It seems they want to bring a form of terror to certain individuals, yet this terror cannot come from physical abuse. That would be impossible, it is the terror of the unknown and the fear of death and the jealousy of life of their victim, they thrive on'.

I remembered all the books on the shelf in Jeremiah's cottage. I went to the window and looked out. I could see that the bicycle had gone, Johnny Onion was probably in the next street selling his wares. Many people were passing leading me to believe an important long-distance train had just arrived at the nearby railway station. The men behind me were talking.

I stood and said, 'And what do you want me to do?' Jeremiah, now a Holy man, answered in a most informative and lucid manner, which I appreciated so much at that moment. 'There is something else. Your father had been told some years ago of a grave where there was a great secret buried within. The dead man's name was famous, yet what was within his grave was not known, but it was priceless. He was gripped with this story. Sid could not get it out of his mind. When he was told by Madame Ella that she could converse with this dead man and find out more of the treasure in the tomb, your father became single minded in this grave search.

We are here, meeting in secret, as to go public with our knowledge and belief is to virtually guarantee ridicule even some form of public order arrest. The police service was one, where I would have probably lost my job once I had brought into the open the reality of what we here have experienced. Even a meeting like this would have brought me into contempt. Look how we all laugh at seances and how priests who attend are mocked'.

I interrupted, 'No, they are not all mocked. Many people I know of attend and take great solace from séance'. I felt I wanted to defend my Dad and the only way at that time was to agree with him. My mind was everywhere.

Jeremiah continued, ignoring my comment. 'Individually, and at another time, we will all convey to you, our personal encounters but none seemed to be as cruel as what happened to your father Eli'. I pondered as their logic. Did they think Dad had thrown himself off the ship or been so frightened his life had meant nothing to him? Who told him about the grave? I looked at the three men individually and there appeared to be a feeling of calm and quiet confidence had come over their demeanours. It was a deep feeling of confidence, and the truth was I wanted to join them and was determined more than ever to find out the truth about my Dad. At the end of the meeting I said goodbye, leaving Jeremiah lodging with Tom and Ron and I walking off in opposite directions.

The walk home that night was a lonely one. I had this strange drawing towards Ron, a kind of needing. I had no idea why. Ron and I had arranged to meet the following day outside the Castle main entrance after our work. The clock tower was the chosen place. I walked the mile or so to the Cottage with a weight on my shoulders. It was akin to a sudden and unexpected imponderable being laid at your door and there was no way out of it. My father, my very own father seeing a ghost, wanting a dead man as a witness to lost treasure. It seemed so humorous that it could have been Music Hall material for a comedian, but the facts were there right in front of me. His chance meeting with Ron, his malady, his close association with Tom and Jeremiah. What about my mother? Did she know? The grave story was fascinating. I knew he was a dreamer at times and wanted more for his family. It seemed an impracticable task to find out. She thinks he was killed at sea by accident, which he probably was, but may there have been another reason, another symptom to add within his behaviour. I only know what I have been told. Then I thought of the meetings in the secretive little corners of the Royal.

I arrived at the Cottage, which was almost empty of clients, the second bell having been sounded. The usual few were leaving in varying states of intoxication. Several of the men spoke to me as I entered yet I did not make out what they were saying. Some women were outside waiting for their men. One woman I knew dreaded meeting her husband from the pub as his manner was aggressive and his meagre wages considerably lessened since consuming alcohol for most of the evening. She was there to assist him home, a duty she did religiously every night. It was a sad situation but not an unusual one.

My mother was clearing the tables of the mounds of cigarette ash and glasses. They knew her to be a fearless lady at closing time. No messing around, they were out! If they lingered their pint glasses were whisked away from under their noses, ash trays emptied, and tables wiped. This domestic activity assured the staff that the lingerer would go and they always did. The sounds of the bolts being shot on the doors to secure the premises soon sounded. My mother did not allow 'after timers' since the demise of my father. It was he who allowed some men to stay, his reasoning being more monies for the till, but it was probably the company and the benign socialising that he enjoyed. Was it one of those men that had told him about the grave? So much to think about. I looked at Mamma. Her tired face showing the strain of a day's duty. I felt so sorry for her and vowed to take more of an interest in her life. After all my brothers and sisters were gone and she had no-one but me. I was of course in full time employ and was happy that she could always rely on me to be her backbone. I wished for a new Bertha.

She was, is and always will be, as far as I am concerned, a member of the family.

Scott Street

## CHAPTER SIX

Yes, I am a powerful looking man, but the outside does not always reflect the inside. I left the brewery to walk to the clock tower and my appointment with Ron. It was not a long walk, in fact a short one, but one of so much interest. I felt threatened, not only by the unfortunates that poked their heads out of dark shop doorways, but the children who pointed to their mouths indicating 'feed me'. It was horrible. The fine carriages and traps clopped away with good gentlefolk, home to their warm and pleasant residences. I wondered how it must have felt to be one of the unfortunates on seeing the rich go to their homes, knowing theirs may be a shared mattress or a leaking shed. On dark evenings, the gas lights flickered both in dwellings and lamp posts. There was no such thing as silence, human habitation was clear to hear. Women shouting at men, men shouting at children and children just being children. Behind closed doors seemed a world of confrontation but of course peace is inaudible. Nearby the dark, swirling waters of the river bringing the coal dust and the filth down from the industrial valleys to the north. I imagined poor people toiling in horrendous conditions to feed the coffers of the wealthy, little knowing that their efforts resulted in the death of rivers as well as hope. One's mind wanders on such walks.

Reaching Castle Street always seemed a success,

an achievement albeit a small one. Many signs of business, with people walking back and fore from the Cowbridge Roads to town. A few men singing after having been relieved of their earnings in some hostelry, two women beggars appeared as ragged piles with their wooden platters empty. I placed two farthings, one in each of the plates. The women hardly moved as though being riddled with afflictions and to move would be painful. Life had been good to me, and I felt I had to put a little piece of my luck into theirs. An impossible dream perhaps but one I believed in. Ron was standing at the base of the clock tower.

When we crossed to the Globe Tavern men were leaving even then, drinks after work, or to escape thoughts, who knows? Sounds of laughter and hi-jinks emanated from inside. On entering I found the usual array of happy and unhappy people doing what happy and unhappy people do well, and that is drink! When the drink is in a person the sense is out of them, and that was only too clear to see in this establishment. Ron and I had agreed that I would do the speaking, as I was a public house person and could resonate with the landlord. Why we were here would soon become known. I crossed to the bar area and beckoned the landlord to speak. I feel it was my sobriety and stance that made the man take notice of me, enough to approach. He was probably in his late forty years of age. His gnarled face showed many a scar of attack with shaving brush and razor. His hair and moustache were greasy grey.

'My name is Eli McNamara, my mother used to run the Royal'. That seemed to impress him, and he pulled me aside into a little 'jug and bottle' type of area. 'I want to ask you about your ghost'.

He looked at me and laughed, 'Well Eli, you don't look the type of gentleman that believes in ghosts'. I wondered as he spoke, what do gentlemen look like who believe in ghosts? Ron followed us and there was a nod between the landlord and him.

I asked a question. 'I have a serious interest in apparitions. I hear through the pub banter that you have seen and heard things in this pub'. It was obvious he was eager to speak and his smile was wide, his eyes constantly on me.

'This pub Eli is one of the oldest around. They reckon a couple of hundred years has passed since it was built. When I moved here, I was told of the grey lady who moved through the walls and drifted down the stairs, but to me it was a laughing matter nothing to take seriously'. He stopped as though waiting for me to answer.

'Have you seen her?' I asked.

'Yes, and my missus, but never at the same time'. I was surprised at his casualness. Ron went to speak but I caught his eye and he refrained.

The landlord looked around at the emptying public bar and raised an arm to a lady behind the bar, which I presumed was his wife. The gesture was reciprocated, and he carried on his conversation.

'I was climbing up the stairs to bed one night when I felt cold, a shiver went through me, as though someone had walked on my grave. I stopped, and then shuddered the shiver away, but on looking up the stairs I saw on the landing, about to come down towards me, this grey woman. I first thought she was some drunk who had got upstairs to steal'.

All this a few months ago would have constituted a laugh but not today. I was deadly serious, and he seemed to reflect that honesty.

'Tell me, did she stare at you first, did she know you were there?' I enquired with some gusto as I needed to understand the motivations and the intentions of the apparition.

'I don't know, I think she stared forward but on coming down the stairs there was no movement, she just drifted. I can remember I wanted to run but I could not. She was wearing a hood and the dress was long. But the scariest thing I remember was her eyes. They were not there! It was just black holes. As she was about to collide with me, I managed to shout, cannot remember what. I pulled my head down to my chest with my hands expecting death. When I straightened up, I looked around and she was gone. I thought I was dreaming or having a nightmare and pinched my arm which hurt'.

He stopped talking as a call for assistance came from behind the bar. His wife was having trouble ejecting two fractious customers. I had seen all this kind of thing before and went across to the bar to see if I could assist. My help was not required. I stayed around as I wanted to know more. I did not even know the name of the landlord, but his story seemed honest and sincere. Ron looked at me and nodded me away and we bade a goodbye.

Standing on the paving outside the Globe Ron smiled and said, 'Sorry Eli, he was probably drunk at the time, or even making it up, as landlords do sometimes. There is no romance in my experience or at the experiences of your father. We must not get into the same bed as legends and whimsies. Those style of ghosties are for the criers for attention'.

I was only just renewing my school day acquaintance with Ron, therefore I did not know him that well, but I did notice a rather pallid and ill look about him, even since our last meeting in Scott Street. He was changing.

I enquired whether he knew more about the grave that Dad had been told about. Ron did know more and was keen to tell me. I suspect he had been waiting for the right time.

We entered the Red Lion public house, which is only a few hundred yards from the Globe, and sat in the saloon bar. We both had blues of ale, which were placed in front of us on a table. Neither Ron nor I smoked which was unusual to the locals in the saloon. The ashtrays were piled up like mountains. In the Royal they would have been emptied into buckets on regular occasions. I compared all pubs to the Royal, this was when Dad and mam were happy together. Ron started to talk in a quiet but confident manner. His story was frankly astonishing.

The Red Lion

## CHAPTER SEVEN

I will relay the story as well as I can remember it, especially the names, which I am sure I have correctly recalled. Many years back my father had met a man casually in the Alms Hotel in town, and they shared niceties and some drinks. They became instant friends and pooled stories. The man, who was Spanish, spoke good English, and he in fact visited the Royal, and had been introduced to my mam. I think he only called in a few times, but it reinforced a strong relationship between my Dad and him. His name was Santos, at least that was the name given to Ron. He had seen him with Dad on the dockside, this on more than one occasion. Santos, told your father an incredible tale about a rogue ship and a hoard it carried. Dad was introduced to other men, and it was in fact one of those who obtained work for Dad on ships running out of the dock. At last I had found out the reason Dad had taken the decision to go to sea. He was lured into it. I remember interrupting Ron at that point to ask a question which had been concerning me a lot. Did Tom and Jeremiah know about what was going on? I also remember very well the long pause before he spoke. Our eyes seemed to hold each other in a stare for quite some period before he turned away. I repeated my question. Did Tom and Jeremiah know about what was going on? His answer was positive, which he then was only too willing to explain. It was as though a great weight was being lifted from him.

'There is so much more to it Eli'. What he spoke of then took the wind out of my sails, if there indeed was any wind left in them! My Dad, Tom and Jeremiah were working together on quests to find lost treasures, one was in a grave in the local cathedral, the other hidden in a wood a few miles to the north.

Then came one of the biggest blows to my comprehension of people's honesty I had ever had. Jeremiah was not qualified as a member of the cloth. It was simply a ruse to gain entry to places he should not be. I remember I pushed my stool back against the wall, finished my blue and asked the landlord for another. Me, a son, a friend, a confident, a gentleman, had been deceived. Ron informed me that he too was a member of the treasure hunting group. My curiosity was beyond anything I had experienced before. I wanted to tell someone, I wanted to run to mother and ask her what she knew. Like a fool I shouted at Ron and told him not tell me any more things about my father. We finished our beers in silence. I walked out and turned north and walked as fast as I could. I did not look behind. I did not want to see Ron.

## CHAPTER EIGHT

Weeks passed and I slowly became cognitive of my late father's secret life. Ron had told me a lot more. With each meeting it became more convoluted and, frankly, incredible.

Back in the 1870s a new steamer had entered the docks by the name of the Weasel. It was owned by a railway company, then sub-let to another, then once again to a London agent. He again sublet to another agent to use. The Weasel was a fast ship which could also carry a few passengers. But in the docks she was loaded with coal, on the instruction of a French agent.

The captain of the ship did not stay aboard but frequented and stayed a couple of nights at the Angel Hotel. He was an affable man who spent his money quite openly and was known as a man who would buy copious amounts of drinks for others. Whilst the Captain was in the finer hostelries of town he met up with a Spaniard, who very quickly joined him on the Weasel as a Subrecargo. This was Spanish for a man taking charge of commercial affairs.

Strange things were going on at the ship down at the dockside. The ship's pantry, the captain's cabin, was being filled with expensive provisions and a large quantity of high-priced bottled alcohol, including fine wines, port and whiskies. When the ship left port, its local pilot stated afterwards to friends that things were very unusual on board. The crew were happy and relaxed in their attitude to life.

The ship then veered off course, did not go to France with its cargo of coal, but steamed down, passing southern Spain to a tiny port. The Subrecargo got off and the name of the ship was changed. She was painted too. The coal was kept on board and used, as if it were bunker coal, to drive the ship as it travelled between port and port. The name of the ship was changed often too. The ship was now travelling around the world and to all intents and purposes, stolen! It reached New Zealand where it was finally seized, and the captain and crew arrested. The owners back in the U.K claimed their ship back. It was an act of piracy, and the crew were jailed.

During the following year the ship, and its story, was told often in town, but then, as with all stories, it was forgotten. The story then leapt many years.

A rich man, a very well-known man in this town, was in receipt of a communication by letter from a prisoner in Spain. The letters which were not easy to comprehend, seemed to say that a prisoner wanted help to recover a huge fortune secreted here. The letter was shown to the Chief Constable who immediately dissed it as deception. The top Magistrate though took a different view. Communications were sent to Spain. After requests for money for his information met with negative answers, the Spaniard wrote this.

He was many years ago a trusted confidant of a Spanish hereditary noble. He was given a large amount of a physical fortune in boxes which he was to hide somewhere in England for temporary safekeeping, to get it away from Spain! He got to London and decided to steal the fortune himself. He made his way to Bristol and then here. He found himself in the centre of town, with a fortune. He smuggled the treasure into the Angel hotel and kept it in his room. He then had a communication from a friend in Spain who told him that he was discovered as a thief, and a team were coming over to get him. He decided to hide the vast fortune by burying it. He hired himself a horse and cart and made his way to a wood on the northern side of town and securely buried the trunk.

This was his witness. Whilst he was staying at the Angel Hotel, he had met a Captain of a ship and with negotiation joined the ship as a subrecargo en route to France. They decided to appropriate the ship and made their way down to a port in the south of Spain. (In my mind the two stories were now gaining credibility and merging as one). Subsequently letters were received by the Cardiff businessman proving the story. There were official letters rubber stamped by the prison authorities and the nobleman. It was noted, during the months that followed, that three men had been observed digging in various parts of woodland to the north of town. The men could not speak English well and were said to be of

Spanish extraction. It is believed nothing was found though. The local businessman was sent a half map, which had been zig zagged, with one side missing. Also, a rough drawn sketch of a building with a straight line coming away from it into a wood.

Over recent years the whole story has melted into obscurity. The other half of the map was not found, nor the exact location. The Spanish prisoner died, and the location of the fortune died with him.

Ron said quite categorically that the wooded place mentioned in the research is unlikely ever to be built upon.

Therefore, if the story is worthy of credence, which it appears to be, out there somewhere is the treasure that Dad wanted to find so much.

There is another comprehensive story relative to this ship. It involves a call at the town docks but not any mention of a fortune.

## CHAPTER NINE

I did not discuss it with my mother, she too was not the woman she used to be. The serenity in awkward situations had dissipated. She snapped and snarled more than gently cajoled. My life had changed, my thoughts were difficult.

Ron's obsession with the recent past was akin to an illness. Indeed he looked ill. It is all he talked about, it gave him pangs of delight and pangs of discomfort, yet his energy never diminished. The day arrived when he was going to walk me to the remains of an old castle and talk of his personal sighting, he knew to be a spirit. I had not realised fully the corrosive effect it had been having on him as he seemed to have weathered the storm extremely well, except I could not understand his loss of weight.

The walk had been a long one, the dappled lane running north seemed endless. The country was beautiful. The density of the colour of the leaves of the endless hedgerow was overpowering. Beech, hawthorn, holly, elder were just a few of the multitude of bushes lining our route. The trees commanded stunning views over the pastures that eventually ended down at the sea. Ron and I were walking away from the sea, and upwards and the climb was wearying. He had done it before and was keen to show me how easy it was. I did not share his competence to climb which he said was needed.

Something was driving him. The idea of a lost castle was indeed fascinating, especially as we were in an area where an industrial revolution had taken place and tens of thousands of people had trod, therefore I was curious.

We stopped and turned around and sat and stared the way we had come. It was a wondrous sight. Stretched across the plain in the mid evening sun was my town. Its buildings seemed to blend into one and gave a piecemeal vision. Far away I could make out the islands and scores of little dots within the sea that could only be ships to and from the docks.

Looking northwards I could see woods and a level hilltop. It was going to be quite a climb.

Ron stood and walked on, again with a most determined gait. The final one hundred yards tested me but not so Ron. He was up the hill and into the woods. He seemed possessed with a vital energy; it had suddenly taken him over. He entered via two old walls which formed a kind of corridor about wide enough to drive a horse and cart through. The walls had no roof and were overgrown with ivy and plant life. There were signs that someone had been at work clearing the site as I noticed piles of scrub and wood debris, yet its overall appearance was of obsolescence.

'There, there, I saw her there', said Tom jumping out from behind a wall. He had an air of enthusiasm as if trying to prove his words via conviction. I walked towards him and stood at the point he had indicated where most of the bramble debris had been stripped away.

'Did you cut this away?' I asked in a kind of professorial way. He nodded as though a verbal answer would have been inappropriate. What was the purpose of doing so?

He did not answer my question but walked away before turning and speaking from some ten yards distant.

'This is where I saw the lady. She was standing there, exactly where you are standing now'.

As Ron spoke, I felt a shiver hit the tops of my arms, not the type of bodily experience I had encountered before, and it frightened me.

'Why did you clear up, I can see no purpose in that' I asked him.

He walked up to me and whispered, 'Because I wanted to see if she could have come from anywhere else. Stupid I know, but a door or a trapdoor to a tunnel. I had to clear that thought from my head. Have you ever been scared or frightened?'

I thought long and hard before I answered.

'Yes, of course I have, many times'.

Ron took a long time to comment again. His stare was cold as he spoke. I had a strange feeling building up in me, not one I had experienced before.

He looked directly in my face, 'I mean terrified, so terrified that the muscles in your body loosen and things happen that haven't happened since you were a babe'. He stared at me. There was a period of silence. I knew what he meant and slowly shook my head back and fore. I have heard about terror but never experienced it. Ron obviously had.

'She came slowly towards me, drifting as though she was on ice. Her face was as white as her dress but her eyes, my God Eli, you should have seen her eyes'. He stopped and stood motionless.

'Go on, go on, what about her eyes?' I shouted.

'They were black', he said in a voice akin to a whisper. 'Black, which made me think they were not eyes just holes into her head'.

I was standing at the entrance to the adjacent walls, clouds seemed to gather above. Ron commenced shaking. It was as violent a bodily motion that I had ever seen. I jumped at him and squeezed him into me to relieve him of the trembling, but it got worse. His strength far belied his weakened frame. I turned him around and saw his face was yellow, the perspiration rolled down over it, his eyes were piercing and staring straight at mine. There was no blink.

I was terrified and let him go, his behaviour turned from shaking into screaming, dropping to his knees he shouted at me, 'Look at her, look at the bloody woman!' I could see no-one yet the tingling I was experiencing caused me to lean tight against an old wall. It was catching.

Ron was staring forwards, away from me towards the interior of the old overgrown castle. 'Stop it, stop it.

Leave me alone'. Those words were said with such power and feeling that I honestly believed I saw a woman in front of me. Ron turned and from his kneeling position I saw a look of terror on his face, a look I had never seen before. I pushed myself away from the wall and grabbed his arm and pulled him, no dragged him, out into the pasture. He ended up face down, I turned him and saw that his eyes were open, the stare was frightening. He was taking in huge gulps of air, then seemingly coughing it out. I lifted him onto his knees then pulled him up to a standing position. He took his own weight and within minutes he oversaw himself.

He sat and said in a puerile way, 'You saw her didn't you. Please say you saw her'.

I shook my head slowly and said, 'No Ron, I saw nobody'. He got to his feet, turned and ran over the scrub and brambles and out into the fields. His terror seemed to have infected me and I ran as if for my life after him. He stopped by an old oak tree, and staring back at the castle ruins, he made me promise not to tell anyone what he had seen. It seems that in his terror he had taken a vow of silence to protect himself from the apparition. Perhaps he thought the ghost, if that is what it was, would get angry if he told of her.

Ron begged me not to tell vicars and priests about the woman. They may try to exorcise the vision as a demon, and then she may come for him! The overriding and forceful thoughts within me were of my father. His slow demise into ill health, his strange death, were obstructing any clean and rational thinking.

I looked to Ron. He seemed a changed young man, even the rosiness in his cheeks a memory. I knew that he was fitter than me, as had just been proved as he ran, which gave me some succour.

It was dark when we reached the black brook and signs of habitation. We had not spoken for many minutes. He seemed to be in control of his senses and apologised for his behaviour. Whatever the reason for the terror that had overcome Ron it had not left him. However normal he wanted to appear I would never forget those moments.

He put his hand out to mine, 'The madding' he said, 'Your Dad called it the madding'. I nodded, the word was unknown to me and I was not going to ask him about my father at that point but, I realised he must have gone through the same hell. The word stayed with me, as did the image. We bade each other a strange goodbye and walked our separate ways agreeing to meet on Sunday after matins at our churches.

## CHAPTER TEN

A meeting of the 'treasure hunters', as Ron called them, was planned for 7pm at Scott Street. I had showed my willingness to be part of it all, I did not want Dad to have died in vain. He was on a quest I wanted, in his memory, to realise it for him. The men knew me well and the same goes for me to them. I was accepted and trusted, and if the truth is known, was fascinated by it all. I did notice that there was a special atmosphere that surrounded me. At that time I did not know why. I was beginning to believe in the treasure. If Dad believed, so would I.

We were all there. The mood was sober and hardly anyone was willing to start a conversation. It was half past the hour of seven and Jeremiah had not arrived at Tom's house. There was a lot to discuss after our enquiries.

No-one would start any discussion without Jeremiah as, in Tom's words, 'We would have to repeat ourselves, and he is the guiding light'.

Jeremiah finally arrived at eight and was full of apologies. I was about to leave and was not too happy with the late start of our meeting. The most notable thing about Jeremiah was his Dog Collar.

'How do I look?' he said in his policeman's voice, which did not become his new calling. The general opinion was positive. I said nothing about Jeremiah not being a real priest. The tea pot was filled, and the cups placed in front of us.

'Now' said Tom. 'Let us start'. 'Eli and Ron have done an amount of research and it appears that every sighting of an apparition is seemingly identical, a female, she has a long flared out dress to her toes, she is average height for a lady. According to one witness in the Rummer Pub she had the appearance of a real lady. What was meant by that we could not ascertain? Sometimes she is wearing a scarf or hat of some kind, other times not. The most striking thing, according to every witness is her eyes, or lack of them. Everyone says they are black holes; she has no eyes'. Tom paused, as though for effect.

'I do not trust every sighting', said Ron, 'It is a matter of belief. Some people I believe are telling us for scurrilous reasons, other want payment of some kind, but there are genuine ones amongst them. I have spoken to men, and it is the men who I believe in most, that describe the same experience as mine. The same terror, the same feelings, the same feeling of power coming from the apparition'.

I interrupted, 'Especially the landlord of the Globe Inn. He saw something?' Ron said nothing.

Jeremiah, who had been listening carefully stood up and fetched a jug of milk from the dresser. 'Can I make one observation at this point? It seems all the genuine sightings that have been reported to us over the months have a distinct pattern. We have a specific ward and staircase in the Royal Infirmary, then the old north castle, the town castle walls, the Rummer Tavern and the Globe Inn. It seems every sighting outside of those are suspect. What is it that draws the lady to all these places, that is what we have got to find out?'

Ron spoke, 'To me the answer is much more frightening, much more disconcerting'.

Ron had refused to say much about his experience before and his reticence caused us all to take little notice. Had he told the truth or was there some exaggeration in the story he had told Tom, Jeremiah and my father.

I recently remembered the outpouring of emotion when a poor lady was hanged in the town prison. It is several years since, but the memory was vivid. I wondered whether her poor tormented soul was loose.

'What turns a dead person into a ghost?' I asked, 'Is it torment, injustice, love, revenge? Surely one thing is for sure, not everyone becomes an apparition. We are just looking for a lady, it seems one lady, as all the descriptions are similar. Perhaps she seeks revenge for an injustice. 'The three men looked at me.

Jeremiah spoke. 'Eli, the dead I fear have a total desire for love, both physical and emotional. They were lost souls in life as well as they appear in death. Love and security were something denied to them, to such an extent it virtually drove them insane. It is one of the main reasons a man of the cloth has to exorcise these poor people, put them out of their hell'.

This information was a revelation to us all as the

reaction was obvious.

We all looked between ourselves before Tom spoke, 'Then perhaps she lived here in Temperancetown, if so then all the bloody women are going to be ghosts'. I smiled which opened the floodgates for each of us to laugh. At the back of my mind was the dead man that Dad was trying to contact and the medium he was using.

At that very moment I experienced uncertainty, far too much information and too many inclusions. We were not at the heart of the conundrum, many decoys to overcome.

There was a sudden ending to the meeting. We arranged another date and left individually to make our way home. Jeremiah was lodging with Tom so I imagined the large pitcher of beer which was always sitting in his pantry would soon see the light of day. Ron walked off. His gait was slow, and I saw his clothes were ill fitting. He had lost even more weight.

I pondered long and hard about the information conveyed by Ron, Jeremiah and Tom. Behind all my thoughts was father. What had happened to him? Treasure hunters was a term Ron had used, but to date it was only he who had communicated that aspect with any intensity.

## CHAPTER ELEVEN

There was something else going on in my life. I had met a young lady. The introduction had been made in the Royal lounge some time before and for some reason as soon as I saw her, I felt decidedly different. There had been many young ladies that had passed my way in the preceding years, none had really inspired me, nor had I walked out with them. Rose was different. She was the daughter of a man who travelled in furniture, a successful gentleman who lived in one of the fine embankment houses within a quarter of a mile of the Royal. Rose often called for her father at the public house around 6pm and they would walk home together. Her father, Mr Isiah Pepler, would have his one pint of beer when he was working the local area. I did not see Rose as just pretty; she was interesting too.

I knew very quickly that she was attracted to me as our eyes would meet, then she would turn away, but not for long. Very soon she was turning to me once more. Rose was drawing me in. Why? Smiles became nods, and words became conversations.

It seems that Isiah Pepler had read the signs and had spoken to Rose about me. He liked me. He liked my ambition, and most of all he liked my father and knew of his sad demise. My move to the Cottage public house did not deter our blossoming relationship.

Rose and I commenced to walk out together,

initially under the strict guidelines laid down by our respective parents, but very soon we were allowed our freedom. I fell in love and so I thought did she. The experience was exhilarating, and we shared all our thoughts on every subject known to mankind. Well, all but one. I did not tell Rose about the treasure hunters and the conversations with Jeremiah and Tom, nor did I tell her of any experiences that had occurred with them. I spoke of the rides on the dray and Jeremiah's cottage but nothing of our conversations. Ridicule is not an emotion I suffer gladly.

Very soon, at one of our meetings in Scott Street, we were going to discuss the lost grave and how we were going to find it. I was curious yet held my own council as far as opening a discussion. I was efficiently and indeed conscientiously, attending to my work. I made sure I always walked the mile or so from the Cottage pub to my workplace. It was imperative I kept fit of body, as my mind was not so.

I was pleased that Tom called at my workplace nearly most days and updated me on any latest news, of which there was none. He was uninvited and there were times I put him off, as I had already pledged to meet up with Rose.

I had bumped into Ron on the way to work on a couple of occasions, sheer chance I presumed. What was obvious to me, therefore to everyone, that Ron was not only losing weight, but he was also becoming more nervous and needy. I could not say with any conviction that I was his best friend, nor of course was I family, therefore his condition affected me more with curiosity than care. His headlong flight from the castle on the hill, the look on his face, had stayed with me.

Tom and Jeremiah always looked tired, yet there certainly were no obvious health worries for them.

I was due to meet Ron after church on the Sunday, and the day before I called to see Tom at Scott Street. It was the short walk of no more than five minutes after work, which I had taken so many times before. The brief dark street of terraced houses looked unflattering in the early evening gloom. Many of the houses had windowpanes stuffed with paper or rags to keep out the drafts. I considered the reasoning for that. One word came to mind, poverty! They could not afford to replace glass, or the landlords could not or did not.

Tom's house did not suffer from such ignominy. It had a very well-kept appearance. I knocked the door to be welcomed in by Jeremiah who turned and walked down the little corridor to the door that led into the rear room, the one with the fire. Tom was sitting there, and he beckoned me to sit too. Jeremiah went to his usual rocking chair, which in days past had been the subject of much mirth. Today though he did not rock in it.

'We are worried about Ron', were the stark words barked by Tom. 'He is in the infirmary'. The words must have struck me hard as Tom carried on his sentence without waiting for my response. 'He's ill Eli, extremely ill. He will not or cannot eat. There are no visits as the fear is the unknown. He has no symptoms that are obvious to the eye and we are told not obvious to the doctor's examinations. He has stopped eating'.

'Why can't we visit him then?' I asked with some concern. Jeremiah moved and as he did, the rocking chair took motion.

'Because Eli, they are afeard of the unknown. A kind of plague'. Jeremiah was not wearing his collar and appeared as I remembered him all those years ago back at his cottage. I could see there was more in his answer than he was telling. I stared at him. 'I am afraid that he may be consumed by the devil. Satan has found a home'.

I wanted to laugh but could almost smell the gravity in the room. Both men were looking down towards their feet and I joined in the silence. Jeremiah rose and stood over me, 'Eli, the last time I saw Ron he said to me, 'What I saw I do not know. Woman or man, I do not know. What I saw though was ugly. It was the last time I saw Ron, but his last words were explosive. He said he felt it take over, possess him. A feeling of instantaneous fright'. I knew of course exactly what Ron had told him was true. Tom beckoned me to sit. Jeremiah poured water from the steaming hearth kettle into a jug and mixed in tea leaves. 'We believe that what has happened to Ron happened to your father. Evil overtook them, causing them to die, purposefully seeking their death to join them in hell'.

'But Ron is not dead', I retorted.

The one-word answer, said with a slow head movement and a stare that terrified me, was 'Yet!'

I looked straight at Jeremiah and said, 'The madding'.

His kindly face turned to ice. 'What do you know of the madding', he shouted. Tom rose and joined him, 'Answer him, who told you of the madding?'

My shock was extreme. Jeremiah moved into my face, 'Eli, who told you of the madding?'

I whispered to him 'Ron', then turned and nigh on ran out into the street and away.

The following day work came hard to me. Concentration was burdensome. The daily clatter of industry in the brewer's environment seemed sometimes non-existent, yet it was there. When I shook my head out of its sombre wandering, the snap and booming of barrels and the whinnying of the gentle giants soon brought me into harsh reality. I really could not go on like this.

## CHAPTER TWELVE

My mother seemed separated from any other form of existence other than the wooden floorboards of the Cottage pub bars. The only use I was within her environment came as a willing labourer; down the stairs and into the flooded cellar to tap the beers. An underwater stream, when in flood, entered the cellar and caused havoc with its arrangements.

Mother had forgotten Dad, or she had dismissed him from her mind. The only good news was that Bertha had been given a job preparing snacks, soup, bread and pickle, or in fact any other thing that needed done in the Cottage. I had not forgotten Dad and I was not going to give in on my friend Ron. I found the idea of giving in so alien to me that it gave me a boost, a sense of direction.

My job was getting in the way of my thoughts. I so wish I could see Ron, get near to him, talk to him, ask questions of him, and perhaps somehow get to the riddle of my father's demise. I was sworn to secrecy within that shameful Shakespeare Club, the fantasy days when my father was my King, and the lanes were my playground had turned. A lot had happened since then.

Tom had called in at my workplace and apologised for his behaviour. I accepted his apology but was still curious. I told him I was calling at the Globe on the way home.

I wanted to clear up the obscure sightings the man

and his wife had claimed to have seen. The short walk from the brewery to the Globe was invigorating as the sights around me took me into another world. That busy world continued as I entered the Globe via the Red Cow Lane door. I pointed to the barrel of my favourite beer, then asked the barmaid the whereabouts of the landlord. She said he was ill and not at work and was upstairs in bed. This information hit me hard into the pit of my stomach. 'What's wrong with him?' I enquired, quite rudely, fearing the worst news.

'Silly beggar fell down the stairs, gone and bust his ankle'.

The news made me smile with relief, which did not go down well with the woman pulling me a blue. I picked up the tankard and sat down in the corner. Around me was a flock of humanity. Tall, short, gruff, scruffy, well attired, fat, thin, laughing or straight of face; not one woman among them. I was pondering whether to continue in my quest of seeing the landlord, when I noticed an older man on the adjacent table. He was smart of dress yet long of whiskers and these were drenched in froth. He was around and about fifty five years of age. I smiled towards him, and he, brushing his whiskers in his sleeve, smiled back. His long hair fell in disarray over the shoulders of his jacket. There was something about this man that kept drawing my head to him, and he to me. It was a moment I will always remember.

A wink from him opened a conversation. 'You're

not a regular here young man?' He questioned.

'No, I have been here just once before. Not for the beer I may add, but I wanted to see the landlord'.

'And did you?'

'Yes, that's why I'm back. I wanted to see him again, but I fear he is indisposed. Broken ankle'.

'Ah, that's what they want you to believe young man'. He sat back and lifted the jug to his mouth and took a long swig of ale. I said nothing but must have looked rather perplexed as he shuffled across and sat next to me. 'Your name Sir?'

'Elijah Llewellyn McNamara' I replied with some pride.

'Your father was the landlord of the Royal eh?' Almost with one eye closed, he turned to one side as if to check if anyone was listening. They were not. I knew my father was well known in the drinking circles, and after all we were not too far away from the Royal, but I wondered what this man knew about Dad. I had never seen him before and therefore he could not have been a regular, or indeed a casual caller to our old pub.

'And what is your name?' I asked. The answer was one I never expected.

'Patrick McNamara at your service Elijah. Sidney was my brother'.

The information was a blow. I never knew my father had a brother therefore, I did not believe it, also the meeting was too haphazard to be true. He sat back pushing against the wall, then bent down to me. 'Eli you're a strapping lad, something I admire in a nephew'. He laughed out loud and sat back down.

'How did you know I would be here?' I asked him, but the answer was only too obvious, 'Tom! He told you'.

'Yes, and he is on his way here also. We thought this may be a good place to further the little problem we have on our hands'. It was if by divine providence the Red Cow Lane door opened and into the public house walked Tom and Jeremiah, vicar's collar, and all. Site of a man of cloth in the pub caused quite a stir and much murmuring, which ceased when he pulled a chair up to us and removed his accoutrement. Tom ultimately joined us after a brief visit to the bar and a glance or two at the barmaid. Her glance back was equally as mischievous.

So, there we were, Patrick my newfound uncle, Tom, Jeremiah and me. The only one missing of our little group was Ron. That thought was repellent to me, poor Ron.

I found out that Tom had written to Patrick in Ireland and told him of the death of my father, and he had been trying to get to our town for some time. He finally came in yesterday on a working ship from Wexford and found Tom in Scott Street, where he had spent the night. My immediate bond with Patrick was now obvious. We were family. His soft Irish brogue and strong character made us instant friends. Tom and Jeremiah kept looking to me and nodding their heads with wide beams across their faces. It was as though the incident of a few days ago never happened. They seemed so happy that Patrick was in town, and he had met with us, and more especially me. The mood changed when Patrick looked to me and said, 'Now lad, we want you to go and see Ron. The Society has lost a member and a visit is imperative'. It appeared he had become in charge of affairs, a man I had only just met, and he a relative! Jeremiah took from his pocket a chunk of rye chew and breaking some off, he passed it around. We sat there in silence for a whole minute, chewing and drinking. I noticed on the adjacent tables the ashtrays were once more overflowing and smoke hung in the air. Nary a sound was heard apart from men pulling on their pipes and dispatching the clouds of shag into the air.

'Eli', said Patrick, 'there is something we want you to do'.

t.

The Globe Hotel

**CHAPTER THIRTEEN**

I stood in the shadows of the long, ornate but gloomy hospital corridor. There was a silence which only comes from previous monotonous noise. It may seem to be a little silly in saying such a comment, but perfect silence, where there has been noise, is eerie to say the least. The hustle and bustle, the comings and goings, the endless chattering of the patients, friends and staff had ceased. For that moment nothing moved. I felt decidedly nervous, so nervous in fact that I moved a yard or so out of the shadows into the dull and uneven corridor light. I wanted to see Ron and it had not taken much persuasion for me to agree to do so. A uniformed porter came towards me. His steel tipped boots hitting the concrete floor with uniformed regularity. The noise started softly but as the man got closer the noise of the boots magnified. He came to a stop alongside me. 'Come on then. You want to see Mr Scrivens. You can't go in, but as long as I stay you can see him through the communication porthole'. I followed along another corridor and into a much smaller one. It had the appearance of what I would imagine a cell block would look like. I heard a moan coming from somewhere in the block. In truth it was more like a loud hum, but it disturbed me.

The man stopped at the second gate on the left of the corridor and twisted a catch on a serving hatch. It fell back to the horizontal and revealed inside a small room with just a low wooden bed on display. There, on the bed, was a man, who did not look up. The warder peered within and shouted, 'Wake up, visitor for just one minute'. I swopped positions with the porter and stared through the opened hatch. It was a large pantry sized room, more like a cell. The light came from a grating across the cell at the end where I believe there should have been glass, but it was absent. I imagined the cold draft and the discomfort. The wooden bed stood only inches from the floor. I saw Ron lift his head, then climb out, to stand. He was gaunt, his skin fell beneath his cheek bones. His clothes were dishevelled and lacking in any cleanliness. His youth had gone. Out of the cell came the most dreadful odour. I could see in the corner a bucket and nothing else. I said the first thing that came into my mind, 'Ron, it's Eli'. He turned and dropping to his knees climbed back onto the bed. 'That's it!' said the porter. He then pulled me away from the hatch and slammed it. 'Follow me'. His voice command was harsh. He marched off. I did what I was told, I followed. I heard the most awful of screams emanating from one of the rooms. The porter took no notice as though it was normality. The scream turned into a form of howling. The porter slowed down to wait for me. We carried on around to the corridor that led us to his lodge and exit.

I walked out into the day. It was raining, the sky was full of cloud and with a distinct feeling of grief, I walked swiftly the half mile north that took me to the Cottage. I entered and seeing the bar empty and my mother out of sight to me, I went straight to my room. My father had lost weight and had changed beyond recognition prior to his last sailing, but Ron had lost his weight in days. He had seen something in the old castle, which made me think what my father must have seen.

I could not wait to get to Scott Street after work tomorrow and see the men. Patrick, Dad's brother, I know had more to say therefore perhaps he was going to explain to me what had happened both to Ron and Dad.

The night was long and made longer as my mother did not tap on the door with her usual, 'Good night, God bless you Eli'. I had got so used to her reassuring blessing that when it did not come it upset me. I know I had changed, most probably with my maturing, and I was aware that my mother had changed. We were becoming distant, and I felt she was to blame. She had lost Dad, she had changed public houses and now I realised what 'the good old days' actually meant. She had lost those too. I blew the little candle out; the flickering remnant had struggled to light the room for some minutes. I lay on my bed thinking. There was one person though that I felt awful guilty about, and that was Rose. I had not written or called to her home. She must wonder what had happened to our relationship.

## CHAPTER FOURTEEN

The walk to work, then testing ales, and sipping ales was becoming tedious. It never used to be. I was happy to be learning the trade of brewer, under specialist supervision. During my half hour luncheon break I wrote a few words to Rose, positive words. I imagined she was not happy with my constant talk of apparitions and visions, therefore I promised myself not to mention anything when I was with her. I would post it at the end of my workday. She did not live too far away, easily within walking distance, but I had an appointment in Scott Street after work, and to me that was much more important.

I pondered as I worked as to the complications of Patrick McNamara, my father's brother. He seemed too good to be true. He did not have any grief written about him. His confidence was one of a Gospeller, a leader, a searcher out of reality, and his appearance in town not one of a mourner. In fact, the more I thought about Patrick the more I was bewitched by him. The way his eyes searched you out and brought you a kind of new reality. He was indeed a distinctive man.

I left the Caroline Street exit at 6pm and there in the little roadway were Jeremiah, Tom and Patrick. They looked a powerful trio, not men to confront either physically or verbally. In truth, their status had grown and grown over the period since my father died, that status was pulling me towards them, the explanation I found hard to grasp. Was the seduction a control? Were they influencing me? They were changing, I did not think I was.

With Tom and Jeremiah either side, Patrick spoke, 'Eli my nephew. We are away to the Globe for an ale. We want you with us'. With that he walked off with the other two following. I hurried up behind them, as they were walking at quite a pace. Why was I doing this? It seems I had to follow.

In hardly any time we had arrived at the Globe and were sitting around a table. The landlord was behind the bar and it was he who served us. It seems his ankle had mended exceedingly quickly. I was curious.

'What was wrong with the landlord then? Anyone know?' The three men looked at each other and Patrick mused, 'Perhaps he'd seen a ghost!'. This brought a smile to my face but not to the others.

The pub was quite full, each table being occupied by several men. In the corner, near the snug, were a couple of women dressed in bombazine and near them on the floor were baskets. Hawkers often had a gin after their work, then they would be off to give the day's takings to a more worthy cause, usually a man.

Patrick offered me a rye chew which I refused. It was Jeremiah who spoke after nodding at Tom and Patrick. 'I hear that my associates here frightened you the other day'.

I knew what was coming and spoke immediately, 'I

would not say 'frightened'. More like shock'.

He looked for reassurance from the others and said, 'We all want to know why you asked about maddings, if you are honest with us, we will be honest with you'. I saw that Tom and Jeremiah were gently nodding in agreement.

I took up my jug and took a swig of beer. 'It was Ron who mentioned it'. The others turned to one another as though a burden had been lifted off their shoulders.

'We were hoping that Eli. Anyone else would have been a serious problem for us. Now tell us why and how he told you'.

I recounted the tale of the happenings at the old castle and Ron's run of terror. I told them that he had just mentioned the word 'maddings', in a sentence but singularly.

'What is going on?' I begged for an explanation.

It was Jeremiah who spoke and told me the following. I use my own words to portray his long speech, which was punctuated with swigs of beer.

Some time ago Dad and Tom, went for an afternoon walk, it was a Sunday and they ended up at the Cathedral. They used sometimes go in and say a prayer, or they would just wander back to the Royal, the cathedral being just a destination, an excuse for a wander. On this occasion they saw two men, not known to them or indeed having the appearance of locals, that were rummaging about among the graves and grass scrub. There seems to have been an exasperation on the men's part as when your father asked if they could help, they were told a rather curious story. There was a kind of pact together one with the other as the men had exhausted their search.

A new world of seeking for treasure then opened for father, a world he had no knowledge of but a world that would soon drive him into near madness. Simultaneously he had met the man Santos in the Alms hotel, where he had been told of a large stash of valuables buried at a location near the red castle. Your father knew the red castle was indeed local and in reality, named Castell Coch. He was told the actual routes that were taken to secure the treasure to be buried. There was even a map, torn in half as an indicator, which gave some form of exact location. The man Santos gave father so much information he could not keep it to himself, and brought in Tom and me, then some others including his brother Patrick. All the names were secret as were the meetings and their findings. Jeremiah finished by saying that the grave search, the red castle search, were by no means dreams, they were reality. Out there were two locations your father wanted to find with a craving that drove him ultimately to his death.

The questions stacked up in my head but only one came out, 'Why did my father go and see a mystic called Madame Ella?'

The reticence to comment displayed an answer

that was not going to be to my liking. I felt it. I knew it. I was told that Madame Ella had spoken to my father across a table, just the two of them, in her rooms in Windsor Place. She showed a keenness in joining him on his search and wanted to contact the spirit world to help them. She told him she would contact the 12<sup>th</sup> century cleric to find out where he was buried. I remember shaking my head in disbelief when I heard of it; I do not now. She told him she could also help him find the treasure in the woods. It seemed most unlikely, but I was aware there was much more to come.

I had enough, I wanted to go home and cogitate on it all. Just before I left, I remember I had forgotten one thing, the word madding. The answer that came my way was highly unpleasant. It was Tom who said, 'When the spirit has taken you over and you are soon to die it is called the madding. Madame Ella warned us, she told us of the madding spirit attention and the insanity that follows'.

I asked the obvious question. 'Did my father shout 'madding?' The positive nod gave me the incentive to turn and leave. Ron was about to die.

## CHAPTER FIFTEEN

On Friday morning, just before I left for work, I was in the tiny corridor that ran between the bars in the Cottage. I was staring in the mirror and straightening my tie, when I heard a knock on the door. I could hear my mother in the kitchen washing plates and glasses, so I answered the knock even though in a rush to leave for work. This door led into little Rose Street, and it was usually for domestic use only. Standing at the door was a man around my age, well dressed, but exceedingly smaller than me in both height and weight. He appeared a little exhausted. He enquired who I was and seemed to show some pleasure when I said my name. He said, 'Mr McNamara, you are to come at once to the city cemetery, something has happened, and they want you there'

His manner was grim and therefore I took his words with the seriousness they deserved.

My answer was abrupt, perhaps too abrupt. 'Why?'

He said he was not aware of the circumstance but simply was told to get to the Cottage as quickly as possible and find Mrs or Eli McNamara. He left and I closed the door and shouted to my mother. She appeared as confused as me but had responsibilities regarding pub opening hours. Our domestic servant, Florence, was instructed to go and fetch Daisy, our barmaid who lived at the end of Rose Street and tell her to come to work immediately. My mother also agreed to send a message via pony and trap to the Brewery. I was going to be late.

I had a bicycle, which I oft times used for work, and it was this I used to get to the cemetery with some haste. The ride was alongside the new boating lake, but I had no time to admire and was soon entering the cemetery via the impressive castle like entry. My mother was to follow in a pony and trap, all being well supplied by one of the pub regulars. Standing adjacent to one of the chapels at the entrance, was a police officer in uniform, a Sergeant, and a group of men, probably around six in number. They were respectfully dressed, except one, who had the look of a graveyard labourer. I laid my bike against a wall and approached the men. One spoke, 'Eli McNamara?'

Once I had verified my name two of the men took me into the chapel and we sat at a table which was laid with flowers, bibles and prayer notes.

'We have some very strange and worrying news for you Mr McNamara'. I remember there was a pause as if waiting for me to speak, but I did not. 'There has been a desecration of your father's grave. It has never happened here before and we are in a complete state of shock. We would like you to accompany us to the plot before we undertake temporary remedial work'.

My face must have been a picture of curiosity. Desecration of grave? My mother had only arranged for a small plot with an equally small head stone to match. 'Best you follow us Mr McNamara'. We made off on foot, joined along the way by another graveyard labourer. No-one spoke, it was unreal. You would expect the walk to be short, it was not. We made along pathway after pathway, turning left then right and onwards. Dad's plot was adjacent to a railway line. We passed one or two people praying on the graves of loved ones, one woman walked past us carrying flowers, no doubt on her way to shed some tears on the earth that covered her beloved.

I saw in the near distance, at my father's grave, a large sackcloth or similar surrounding it.

'Prepare yourself for a shock son' the grave labourer said, but I certainly was not prepared for what I saw. We walked behind the sackcloth barrier and there where the neat mound of the grave once was, I saw a hole. A long and very deep hole. My whole being was one of disbelief, an emotion that I was becoming more and more aware of, but this was different! No-one spoke, which made matters worse. The earth was in neat mounds around Dad's plot, but the most horrific of thing was the casket. The top had been lifted off and lay alongside at ground level. I peered down into the darkness, where the sun could never reach unless overhead. Dad was gone! I thought it, then shouted out loud, 'Where's my father? Good Lord tell me where my father's gone?' One of the men put his arm around my shoulder and pulled me back away from the drop into the grave. I pushed him off. 'Where is he?' I screamed at them. The men grabbed me with quite physical force and held secure. The sight and the sound brought several people towards us. Their inquisitive nature probably enhanced by a desire to assist. I wanted no help, I wanted answers. 'Where is my father's body?'

'Body snatchers' said the grave digger, which brought a huge admonishment from the cemetery officials. He was told to shut up in no uncertain terms.

'The simple answer is Mr McNamara; we do not know. There has never been anything like this before and we honestly do not understand what is going on. If it is a body snatcher, it is the first and why your father?'

I pushed him away and went back to the graveside and kicked earth around looking for things, what I do not know.

I looked down one of the endless pathways and saw a police officer approaching and with him my mother. Things were about to get worse.

For some reason, my mind went back to a wild weather night when I was a child. Seeing my mother approaching recreated a past image, an image that was gone in a moment. The past, where the wind was howling outside a sea cottage window, drafts were fighting their way between the sheets and the bedroom fireplace was empty and cold. It was only my mother coming into that wee bedroom that made me feel safe, the howls of the wind disappeared, and I felt secure with her nearby. I was a child, now I am a man, but that feeling returned, this time though with no warmth and no escape from my situation.

As she approached the sackcloth barrier the policeman pulled away and the officials did also, but not before pulling back the grave labourer who they thought may not adhere to grave etiquette. The moment she went behind the barrier a goods train chuffing and clanking up the gradient, blew its whistle. I went to her, and it was just the two of us standing at the grave that used to contain the body of my father. I stood my ground, but Mam took a couple of steps to be alongside the empty grave, she bent down and scooped up some earth which she gently sprinkled into the hole. She looked at me and lo and behold Mam was smiling. Her face seemed to light up as the grin became more and more apparent. She walked out and back along that endless footpath between graves. I ran after her, leaving the others at graveside. 'Mam, Mam' I shouted, 'Talk to me, please talk to me'. She stopped and turned.

'Eli, your father is where he wants to be. You take great care my son. You take great care'. With that she hurried off, leaving me dumbstruck. For the first time I noted there was fear in her face. The policeman, who was following, halted adjacent to me, and shouted towards Mam.

'Mrs McNamara, Mrs McNamara, you have to make a statement'. His words fell on deaf ears. I walked in Mam's direction. The officials came running after me, and we all made our way back through those dismal walkways to the chapel. Even the posies of flowers and laments of some mourners could not bring me back from those words, 'Eli, your father is where he wants to be'.

Mam knew, Tom, Jeremiah and everyone else knew what was going on but me. Dad appeared to have lost his mind, perhaps even lost his soul, to greed and the omens of another woman. I wanted reality, the ordinary, the uncomplicated, and the only place to find that was in my workplace.

## CHAPTER SIXTEEN

It was 5pm and work had been a distinct displeasure, and not the relief I was expecting. Concentration was lacking and the people around I regarded as a nuisance rather than comrades and helpers. I was not proud of that but could not shake myself out of it. This nightmare that was going on inside my head seemed to be taking me to the most ridiculous of thoughts. I suspect anyone in my position would feel that way, but I honestly believed that my world was not real. There was a kind of parallel one outside there watching me. I kept swinging around at the slightest noise, as though to catch a glimpse of it. What that something was I did not know. Five o clock could not have come quick enough.

I was beginning to fancy and look forward to an ale. I had seen so much of that in the Royal where the men were literally queueing as the doors were opened. It was their medicine of choice, an antidote to the miseries of the day and more importantly of their life.

I was pleasantly surprised. As I walked through the gates into the street there stood Rose. Her shiny auburn hair was stuffed inside her bonnet, yet some still managed to fall on her shoulders. In that instant I knew I must do all I can to keep Rose in my life. It was not her loveliness that was paramount in my mind but her common sense and downright uncomplaining attitudes. I think she must have seen my face brighten as hers reflected it. Her smile was a tonic that I lapped in. 'Hello, I'm so glad to see you'.

She came to me and pecked me on the cheek with her lovely lips and said. 'And me you. Come on let us go to a Tea Shop and have a chat. I want to tell you something'. She did not have to ask me twice as we breezed hand in hand along into the main street and Purnell's. This was a Tea Shop we had used before, and I knew to be a refined and special place. It was Rose who found a little table for two in the corner, away from any neighbouring ones, therefore not being overheard, which pleased me deeply. The next half an hour was quite idyllic, a needed escape, we seemed to get on so well once more, the flame was burning brightly. Her company bucked me up, so low was the day, so high the evening.

Rose, finishing her personal pot of tea, put her hand across and onto mine. I was still in a light mood, but I saw her smile had melted away. 'Eli, I have something to tell you'. I gently pulled away from her grip and sat back into my chair, but this only prompted Rose to lean forward more. 'I have been thinking a lot of what you told me about your father, and those morbid and frightening thoughts you were having. I realise that I was a little unpleasant to you, as it was all such a new world to me'. I smiled in agreement but said nothing. 'I have a friend in chapel who has been to see someone, someone who is dead'.

In a blunt display of anger, I stood up which caused

Rose to sit back onto her chair. 'What?' My shock at such a comment caused my temper, but I sat back down and said nothing.

After an awkward moment Rose said, 'I have a friend Eli, who last week attended a séance in town. She said that the mediums brought her dead grandmother back into the room and she could ask questions'. I just stared. The silence between us must have lasted a minute or more.

'So, you think that will help me, do you?' My tone was dismissive, which was rude, as I know she was trying to help.

'Yes, I do'. Her sincere answer made me concentrate and think a little more deeply than I had.

In truth I wanted to know more. 'Go on'.

'My friend is called Elizabeth and she was quite distraught when her gran passed on a few months ago. She was finding it hard to get over it, as her gran was a special part of her life, and much loved. She was advised to go to a séance in Windsor Place, just off the main street in town'.

The location hit me hard, a location I was now aware of. I decided to say little about my knowledge and act as though it was novel to me.

'I know it', I retorted, 'Very nice houses there, quite a knob's street'.

Rose nodded and carried on, 'Well she went one evening at half past seven with her mother. It cost her two and sixpence which her mother paid. They spoke with grannie'. At that moment, the charming little waitress approached and informed us that the tea shop was closing, and did we want any more before they locked up. I indicated that we did not. Rose stood and I crossed to retrieve her coat from the main row of hooks, which by now were empty. We had not noticed, everyone was gone. Outside in the street we stood in the doorway, and I heard the bolt being shot across.

The day's business was over. 'I'll walk you home' I said. My intention then was to hail a cab to return me through town and over to the Cottage. I was late and I suspect my mother may be wondering where I was. Things were so distressing now, and any little thing was upsetting us both. As we walked, I became more and more interested in the séance. We reached her home, and we noticed the curtains move, which made us both smile. Rose's Mam liked her home in the house, away from any bad influences, and to me she was a worrier beyond the normal, but there was love behind it. During our walk I informed Rose that I would go and look for the house in Windsor Place and made a pact with her that if I did go, I would take her. Perhaps the closeness of our new relationship was skewing my senses, but I did indeed want to see, and I was not going to go on my own! My father had been enchanted by Madame Ella and I wanted to know why.

In the days that followed I found out that just

across the road from my workplace was the old waxworks, and up a long set of stairs another medium was at work. There had been many reports of crowds of people waiting to go in, but I was told that this phrenologist only spoke to one person at a time. It was in the evening that a Madame Keithley held séance sessions, and it was a maximum of sixteen persons who could take part. My wise head, from my mother, pushed me in the other direction as far as contacting the dead was concerned, that is stay as far away as possible from your home or workplace. It would be an added complication if I were confronted by a close friend around the same séance table.

I sought out the Windsor Place house and found that it was a basement at number 12 that the seances were held. The few steps down to the lower ground floor, under the fine town house, led to a black wooden door. There was a basement window, which looked out onto the steps, but this had been boarded over. It was a woman who was the link between the dead and the living and it was she who opened the door when I knocked. Her appearance was majestic. A fine-looking lady of no more than 50 years of age, her clothes were dark as her hair. The most striking thing were her eyes, black with a glint in each that seemed to penetrate. I remember I felt disturbed by her, simply because of those piercing eyes. Was I looking into the same face that had captivated my father? I introduced myself and asked detail concerning the seances she held. She did not invite me in but gave a lengthy sentence referencing the event and how I book. She also asked me many questions about myself and my life. I used Rose's surname, as she had requested. I did not mind that at all, one or the other, it was all the same.

Madame Ella informed me she had to ask pertinent questions to make sure I was not a waste of her time, a religious zealot or a disbeliever who would upset proceedings. It did not take me long to prove to Madame Ella, as she called herself, that I was genuine. I told her my father had recently been killed at sea and I missed him greatly. I was aware of another person inside the basement moving around, but at that stage I did not know whether it was a man or a woman. I remember asking one important question to Madame Ella that she seemed to take great notice of. 'Outside of your environs do you believe in ghosts?' It was a rather childish question coming from a big man like me, but it hit a nerve.

She stared and those eyes seemed to trap me, the glare was gripping. 'There are no ghosts', she snapped. 'My visitors are from the nether regions of the universe. Our dear departed manifest themselves through me. A visitation is only achieved by power, the power of a special person. I am one of those special people. Dead people need supernatural access to enter and leave the world of the living. Ghosts, haunted castles with secret corridors are spoken of by charlatans'.

She certainly did not like my enquiry, which concerned me. I told her of Rose, and that she was my lady friend, and both of us wanted to attend. It seemed my identity was to her satisfaction and arrangements were made for Rose and I to attend at 12, Windsor Place at 8pm in exactly one weeks' time. I could not wait to tell Rose.

Another thing I liked about Rose was her reliability. I knew that when I said we would meet at quarter to eight-o-clock on the corner of Windsor Place and Queen Street, she would be there! On that exact point of time, I saw her walking towards me. I had arrived a good ten minutes early as I wanted to get some form of positive belief. I walked up and down the street at speed which took my mind off morbid thoughts and acted as a kind of normality, considering the strange position I would soon be in. I hugged Rose. It was the feel of a man who was about to protect a woman from something improper or odd. She hugged me even tighter which brought a sort of explicit masculinity to me. I smiled the smile of a man without a care in the world. The truth was I was far from confident and was concerned at what we were about to experience. Rose though was becoming full of fun and seemed as though she did not have a concern, even though we were about to speak to the dead! She was oddly excited which was the reverse to me; I felt frightened and apprehensive.

As we approached the basement steps we

noticed a small group of people, all from the better classes, nearby. We held back at about fifty yards away, until two of the people, a fine gentleman, and his lady, made their way down the steps. Rose and I formed the last two in the queue. As we went through the basement door, a rather large and very well-dressed man in his 60s, pulled it shut behind us. He had the largest set of whiskers I had seen in many a long year, which I thought added to his authority.

This was it! I felt a shiver, and just for a moment I regretted my decision to agree to this. There was a musty smell of damp, probably from somewhere deep in the walls, but as the light was negligible, it was only the smell that my senses had picked up. To be in the presence of the dead was not a daily experience and I was unexpectedly anxious. I noticed the sparkle of anticipation had gone from Rose. She was nervous as me. I was not to know then, but the next hour was to detonate a crisis and a void in my relationship with Rose.

## CHAPTER SEVENTEEN

We walked into a large and dark room where black curtains were hanging against the walls giving a crypt like appearance. The window in the room, which I had seen boarded up from the outside, did not appear to exist within. It gave the impression of a plain, curtained wall. There were seats arranged in four rows of four chairs; none of the seats were touching each other. They pointed towards one wall, and in front of that wall was a table. The woman I know as Madame Ella was sitting behind it. No-one spoke. The room was illuminated by burning candles on little shelfs which were no more than six inches in length. There must have been a dozen of them, the flickering adding to the expectancy of the occasion. There seemed to be a lot of shuffling around by the newcomers, which included us, but little real noise. The distinguished whiskered man who had met us at the door, made sure we were all seated properly. I was not put next to Rose. That would have surely disturbed her. Then Madame Ella stood. The vision was not good. Behind her was a large candle, which burned brightly, and surely gave everyone at the meeting a surreal feeling; I know it did me. There were some who had clearly been before, their look of serenity was not matched by mine, or indeed Rose's. In the half-light she looked a little ghostly, if I can use that expression.

When everyone had settled down Madame Ella nodded her head up and down several times and said, 'Mr Davies, you can leave us now'. I heard the door close gently behind us. So, there we all were. Silence reigned. In that minute I thought of mother, home in the Cottage serving the beers to the men and gin to the women. What would she have thought of this? Then I started to question why I was there. What would Dad have of thought of me?

Madame Ella spoke, 'Good evening everyone'. She waited whilst there were muttered responses from all present. 'We are here to communicate with a long-lost sister, a father drowned at sea and anyone else that your thoughts may summon. Are you all ready?'

There was a kind of synchrony in our answers, as though we were at a small children's school. 'Yes, Miss Ella' 'Yes' 'All ready, thank you Madame', were some of the retorts.

Were we really going to speak to my father? She left the table and walked around the room cancelling each candle with a snuffer. Slowly, with each snuffing, the light dropped, but the atmosphere grew in anticipation. I felt a drop in temperature which brought on a noticeable shudder within me. I spotted a gentleman in front of me lean across to hold his lady's hand. She pushed it away.

There was a slight shuffling which ceased when Madame Ella spoke. 'First, we must all relax, all clear our minds of the day's routines; they have gone. We are now! We are one group. We are safe in this group, in this room. Let us sing together, as we always do, perhaps a hymn, one we all know. Everyone must sing, whether your voice is discordant, weak or powerful, we will sing'.

I was not expecting this at all. 'Before we do so I will sing alone. This hymn is more than fifty years old, and I have heard it sung only once, and that by an American lady who attended here. She had stood, as though raised up by spirits, and sung on her own. The hymn was a key, a key to another world. It opened the door then to her and it will open the door now. It is called 'One day, dear children, you must die'.

This was addressed to an audience that by now was not only excited, but perturbed. The woman and man in front of me, turned to each other, I could see the movement in the light of the candle on Madame Ella's table. A man was shaking his head. Why I do not know.

I had the mistaken impression we were going to sit around a table, perhaps with our arms outstretched, but it was nothing like it. Madame Ella commenced to sing a morbid and depressing song, this in a voice that was husky and dragging out each word, as though it was her last. I was becoming frightened; the darkness, the room, the song was unreal. I felt alarm building inside of me, when after the last line she threw her head into air and ordered us to sing a hymn, any hymn. Her manner was so persuasive that I started to sing a Christmas hymn, 'Once in Royal David's City', others mumbled hymns. It was an unpleasant cacophony of sound that steadily grew louder and louder as each tried to outdo the other. I had never heard such a noise ever before! Whilst we were singing, she walked around the perimeter walls of the room, stalking like a wolf ready to pounce on one of us. I looked across at Rose. What she was singing I do not know, it was lost in the awful din. Madame Ella was back at the head of the little audience and raised her hand and screamed out the command, 'Stop!' The deathly silence that followed was as frightening as the row that preceded it.

I stared forward at a surreal sight. The woman in a long black dress with a black bonnet was staring straight at us. No, it was more like right through us! This stance was maintained for what I thought were many minutes, but probably seconds. I heard a muffled whimper from somewhere in our sixteen. My inclination to smile had gone, now it was to hold the hand of someone near to me, a movement I dare not make. The Madame slowly faced the direction of the whimper, an elderly gentleman, just in front and to the left. She was now holding the candle in front of her face. Her stare was enough to frighten even the hardiest of people present, her shadow jumping around the room with the vagaries of the draught on the candle flame. I then heard a single bell. It was more akin to a tinkle and seemed far away.

Her head shot forwards again. 'Listen, listen' The

words were snapped out in a whispered voice. 'Now stand'. We all did, some very slowly, some as quick as an army soldier. 'Listen'. The order was whispered and drawn out. 'Light, they do not like the light'. She blew the candle out which left the room pitch black. We could not see a thing and it was extremely unnerving. I hoped that Rose was being wise and realising that within an hour we would be on our way to our respective homes. Madame Ella started to chant, 'Yes, yes', others joined in, their voices low, some whispered. To my right I saw a strange shape coming out of the wall. It had the appearance of a bouquet of flowers and was above standing head height. It moved along the wall, went dark and disappeared. I held my breath. I know there was a wall there, and there were no other persons in the room other than we seventeen. The man, Davies, had left through the only door and Madame Ella was at the front table. A candle was lit and put down onto the table. It threw light upwards across the woman's face and against the wall. The shadow seemed alive. If it was supposed to appear frightening it certainly worked. She had the appearance of a witch.

'I hear someone coming. I hear someone coming'. Her words were said in a way that I am sure no-one was about to disbelieve. I will admit at that moment I was excessively scared. A bead of perspiration ran down my cheek, as if a tear. I felt for Rose, she sitting next to strangers. I could not even put my arm around her. A pinging of a bell brought a reaction in me. There was a strange prickling at the back of my legs which continued then on up to my arms. The whole occasion was madness.

Unexpectedly the woman threw her head back with a jerk, and in the solemn gloom I could make out her mouth moving, this corresponded with a groan, as though magnified in a tunnel, coming from somewhere, in which direction I could not grasp. I was by now clutching on to the arms of the chair, as were the others present. It was a new experience and a dreadful one. The groan turned into a man's voice, deep and resonating all about the room. The woman said gently, 'Are you there? Who is that? Who wants to speak with us?' There was no answer, but the silence was broken by snippets of nervous apprehension in the audience. The words, if that is what they were, decidedly unintelligible.

A man then spoke in a slow and emphatic manner, 'Ruby, ruby. It is me Tom'.

A woman in the seat behind me shouted out 'Tom, are you there, Tom? Are you there? Yes, it's Ruby, I'm here Tom'. The voice of the man had corresponded with the open mouth movements of Madame Ella. My God, a man had taken over the woman! I heard movement from a seat behind me and then a shout, 'Tom, speak to me Tom'. Madame Ella leant forward into the glare of the candle, 'Sit down, please sit down. Any movement and the exchange is broken'. Abruptly my eyes became used to the contours of the room, and I could see Madame Ella and everyone else. I was startled and wondered how they had done this. It changed quickly to an extremely bright beam that had the appearance of sunlight. Impossible, it was almost night-time, and I was underground. The magic feel of the sunlight turned into horror as I looked around the room. The group were transfixed and staring forward at Madame Ella. It was only me who could see the light! I attempted to speak but heard nothing. I knew I was shouting but still no-one looked at me or moved. To the right of Madame Ella, in the far corner of the room, I could clearly see a man. He had a blackened face and was dressed in black. He had a little megaphone and was asking to speak to Ruby, he wanted to reassure her that he was alright. I could see Rose. She was leaning forward and engrossed in the events of the night. I tried to call out to her or touch her, but I failed, she could not hear, nobody could hear me. I was in absolute disbelief at what I was experiencing. My senses were being attacked from all sides. I was alert, so it seemed I could see and hear all that was going on in the room, yet I could not speak! I felt terrified and stood bolt upright, as if frozen to the spot.

As the intensity of my terror increased, I was drawn to another new light. Where that light had entered from, I did not know, but the light had shape, a human shape. There standing in front of me was my father. His clothes were not discernible, but his head was. I was transfixed, my face burned as though scores of pins were being pressed in. I felt weak, and my heart was pounding so hard I thought it would either stop or leave my body. The pain was deep, I could hardly breathe, and my arms were now stuck to my sides, I was paralysed. I had also become so cold that it penetrated to the very core of my being. Was this the transition from life to death? My father's form floated towards me. I wanted to run away, but could do nothing, then he smiled, and I saw he had no eyes, my God, he has no eyes! I yelled for the Lord to protect me. The smile was now ingrained into me, the intensity complete. It was the look of evil and like no other. My God it is hate! I tried to back away, but he kept slowly coming. Dad was so close to my face I could see into the black holes that once were eyes. My being loosened and my arms and feet became mine again. I punched, I kicked, I shouted. I could hear screams. I fought for dear life to get out of the room, nothing mattered other than escape. Chairs fell or were kicked over. The room was alive with noise, the commotion ear splitting. I was fighting, my only thought was to get out, to escape. I heard Rose yelling my name over and over again. Then she and the noise was gone.

Nurses in their distinctive dresses appeared, and walking towards me at a swift pace, a man of the cloth. I did not recognise him. I tried to stop him and communicate as though he was my saviour to rid me of that awful apparition. He walked right through me.

# CHAPTER EIGHTEEN

I woke. The room was dimly lit, so dimly lit that my eyes took a minute or so to fully focus. I was lying on the floor and looking up at a white ceiling, limewash white. The walls were the same colour but the floor was a greyish concrete. The light was coming from a small wind hole high above in the end wall. The room had the appearance of a cell. The deep brown and gnarled wooden door had an iron drop down hatch. It was black and shut tight. I stood up and turned around and around on the spot in my cell. Where was my mother? How had she allowed me to get into a place like this? I heard a scream. It was not the scream of a woman but that of a man. Somewhere near there was life, but what kind of life? Obviously human and deeply upset. I then heard another shout. 'Shut up!' The screaming ceased. There was real life in the occurrence close by, what that was I do not know but was to find out. Humanity must prevail and feed me, water me. I needed water so badly. I looked around my room. If I did drink water, there was no privy where I could lose it later. I shouted out just one word at the top of my voice, 'Help'. I waited for a few seconds then heard the same voice again, 'Shut up!'

The iron door hatch slammed open to reveal a face peering through. A man with a black moustache yet auburn whiskers. 'What do you want?' said in a deep and penetrating voice.

'Where am I?' I asked.

In fact, they were the first words that came into my mind but what I really wanted to say was 'Where is my mother?' As the man did not answer I said those exact words, 'Where is my mother?' The hatch slammed shut and I heard the echo of boots walking away. Another scream close by and then silence.

I was in a madhouse! The realisation was helpful. I had a direction in life, to get out of here! The life I had seen in the shape of the moustachioed man was the shape of the real world outside. It was he I must court and learn from. He will be the conduit to my mother and normality. Such simple thoughts for a man in such a difficult position.

My eyes now were fully used to the gloom, and I looked around the tiny room. I saw some scribbling but could not make it out, even if it was in the English language. Also, more concerning to me, were reddish stains near the cell door. They were blood, or at least the remnants of blood that had been scrubbed into the spaces between the sturdy brickwork.

Days passed, I presume nights too, which is rather flippant. I could not tell. I started a methodology based on food. A kind of porridge meant it was breakfast time and so on. In the corner of my cell was a wooden pail where I did my business. The smell was becoming overpowering, and I was determined when the hatch opened next to ask for some form of hygiene in my toilet.

When it opened for the daily pitcher of drinking water to be pushed in, I rushed up and asked for the pail to be removed or changed. The hatch slammed shut. I sat back down. I did not feel well but knew it was pointless to complain as there was nothing but heartlessness afoot in the building.

A strange feeling came to me. I was aware I was sitting down but my body was up and moving. The fright was instantaneous. I appeared to go right through the door and found myself on the other side in the world of the moustachioed warder. Along the corridor was marching a scraggy little man with long hair and what looked like a sack for his dress. He wore no shoes. Manacled to him was a warder. The man was carrying a pail and they both stopped at my cell door. If they had seen me they took no notice at all. I saw the warder open the gate and push the scraggy man in. Now came one of the most disturbing and explosive episodes of my life. I could see myself sat on the wooden bed! I saw the man lift the soiled pail and put down the new one. The warder then dragged him out of the cell and slammed the door shut. They marched off down the corridor. My dear God, I was in two places at one time!

Why my mind was registering this I do not know. The questions were coming at speed. My movement was now preventing me from concentrating. I had started to spin, very slowly at first, but as I spun faster my world became bigger. All around was space, wide open bland space as far as my tired eyes could see. It would be impossible for me to recollect or understand what happened. I fell, where to or from I do not know.

My eyes gradually opened. My first thoughts were, please, please someone, make me normal. Who I was pleading to I do not know, but would suspect the good Lord or my mam? I remember opening and closing my eyes hoping that my view of life would change. It was something I had done often as a child lying in bed in the Tudor. Close, open, close, open.

I was in a hospital style room alone. The room was gloomy and small, one light was burning. There were no windows, and I was lying on a bed, fully dressed. There were various medical notices attached to the walls. The room was tiled green to a lip halfway up the wall, then a dirty colour of cream. Next to me on a small table was a pewter jug of water and a tankard. I poured myself a drink then got up and tried to open the single door. It was locked! I was a prisoner. It was then I remembered Windsor Place. Where was Rose, Madame Ella and the others and my Dad, my soulless Dad. I panicked and started running around the tiny room as though a mouse looking for its hole. I shouted for my Mam. I wanted her so much.

I banged on the door and soon a key turned in the lock. It opened and standing there was a religious gentleman holding in front of him a small wooden cross. Standing behind was my mother, my loving mother. There were others behind her. Men dressed in uniform.

The priest walked into the room. I sat back on the bed and attempted to speak and ask the question which was running around my head, 'Where am I?' The Priest held the Cross over me and started to chant. My mother attempted to come around the gentleman, but he held his arm out preventing her. She did not resist this. He lay a white cloth over me and pulled it up over my face.

'God almighty. I cannot see! God help me! I am not dead. I kept repeating I am not dead, but no-one heard. To all and sundry I was mute, the words I was trying to utter were not coming out of my mouth. There was no movement in my body. My father in the corridor was appealing to me for help which I did not give him. It did not make sense. My head was hurting, a painful and horrid hurt. I was dying or dead! The Priest had given me the last rights. Why had they left me? Why had they closed the door? Is this what death is like? An awareness. Hadn't they seen me walk from the door and get onto the bed? Had I imagined that? I was in a half slumber, a kind of a suspended life. I must appear dead, even though I am not. What had my father done? He had magicked some sort of spell. He was trying to get me to join him. This thought inspired a new attitude. A deep instinct I presume for survival. I attempted to explode every muscle in my body, arms, legs, fingers, toes and the most important, my mouth. I wanted to speak and hear my own voice.

I opened my eyes. It may seem a simple thing to do and to accept. It was not! My eyes were closed under the shroud cloth. I heard the door unlock and then the tiny creak of it opening. Hands touched my head and pulled the shroud down away from my face. In a flash I opened my eyes. Confusion reigned. I saw a nurse, the metal tray she had been carrying clanked to the floor. Her face in mine yet frozen. I reached out to touch her. She screamed and ran out of the room slamming the door behind her. I kept pushing and pushing muscles and opening and closing my eyes. I heard my own voice at last and became aware of my prostrate position on the bed. The door opened again. A doctor entered followed by the nurse. I turned my head slowly to one side and without blinking stared at them.

'My God in Heaven! This man lives.' I heard the doctor's words clearly as he pulled the white shroud from my body. At that moment I must have become unconscious as when I woke the room was a hive of activity, and there, standing with her back to the door was my mother. I called to her and she rushed to me and we hugged. I felt the delicious and content feeling of love and security. I was safe.

## CHAPTER NINETEEN

Within one week I was home and in my bedroom in the Cottage. I kept telling myself I was normal. I had been told I collapsed with a seizure of some kind, which to all intents and purposes was so bad, it led the medical professionals to classify me as 'dead'. Strange, so strange.

After a few weeks I was classified by the doctor as safe to carry on a normal and productive life. For that I thanked him. I could not find either Ron, Tom or Jeremiah and decided to confide in my lady friend, Rose. She was in the séance; she saw what happened. I had a theory which was so farfetched and, even to me, so ludicrous, that I had to discuss it with someone. Rose was the one.

I believed that the apparition I had seen in the corridor, which turned out to be my father, had attempted to take me into his world beyond life. His attempt had failed because I deem the knowledge I had gained from Tom and Jeremiah acted as a shield and reflected Dad's attention.

I had written to Rose and as a result we met in the St Mary Street coffee shop we had frequented some time before. My letter to her had realised a quick response and a meeting was arranged.

My conversation with her was a long one. Her comments predictable yet I thought I perceived a glimmer of empathy. I am sure that Jeremiah would verify these gloomy goings-on, and then she would understand.

I am afraid her empathy was little more than pity. She appeared a little distant and did not appreciate my 'temporary insanity' as she called it. I had scared her. She told me what happened in the séance was not too hard for her to classify. I had gone berserk; the occasion had got to me, yet no-one else had experienced the terror. I told Rose that I had seen the man who was working alongside Madame Ella and how a deception was taking place. She made it clear she did not believe my observations; they were just excuses for my behaviour.

Over the following weeks I could see a distinct coolness in her manner towards me. Whereas we were often as one in humour, interests and sweet talk, now there was a distancing. Her infectious and bubbling laughter was no more. We were drifting apart. My heart stayed with her but in truth I knew her heart had grown cold. In my long hours in bed I thought how foolish I had been to convey my thoughts to her and my regret was total. Imagine my surprise when she arranged a coffee shop meeting, then asked if I wanted to go away for a couple of days for a holiday? Rose was visiting a lady friend whom she was to stay with. A train ride, a night in a room in a small hotel for me, maybe an attempt to rekindle our relationship. It was indeed a shock, but a pleasant one.

## CHAPTER TWENTY

Every part and direction in my life was now a constant battle. My enthusiasm for employment, my general feeling of wellbeing and ambition waned each day that dawned. The feeling that I was mentally sick tore at my mind, and my energy sapped so much until I found rising in the morning a chore of chores.

I was aware during my life in the Royal that old men had strange minds, their memories diluted, their conversations wandered from one strange sentence to the next. Some just sat there with their mugs, staring and not wanting to acknowledge anyone. It appears age brought peculiar opinions and behaviour. I was not old, yet I was displaying every indication of senior years. My body was the same as ever, but I could not break through the froth that my mind had become.

I cannot tell you what everyone else in my life was doing, achieving, or saying. I had only one thought, my dad.

After seeing Rose I was purposefully avoiding Tom, Jeremiah and my uncle. They were the spark to everything bad in my life. I felt evil towards the ridiculous treasure hunters, the cathedral grave treasure, the buried treasure in the woods. I wanted a pure and beautiful escape from it all, yet I did not want to be alone.

Then bad news came my way which threw me into a panic. Ron had died! The madding had taken its victim.

The news hit me hard and in truth horrified me. I did not want anything to do with his funeral or his family, I came first. The madding was not going to take me!

## CHAPTER TWENTY-ONE

Our destination was Cardigan. I can tell of my experiences, as the effects were minimal, yet it should have been quite the opposite. Rose's friend was to meet us at the station, and she was to accompany us on sightseeing experiences. The train journey had been long, perhaps the longest I had ever taken and I was tired. We changed at Whitland Station. This was the last of the changes. We made our way over a pedestrian bridge and onto the correct platform for the journey up to Cardigan. I had been warned this was going to be a slow train, probably two carriages, and even a cattle truck or two. My instructors on this were two rather portly gentlemen who had accompanied us in the same compartment for the whole of the previous journey. They were staying on the train to go even farther west, but we were now due to go 'a kind of northwest' as the gents informed us. The little train duly left for Cardigan and the experience was decidedly different, this was because the people travelling with us were country folk and speaking in their local Welsh vernacular. The chuffing of the locomotive was a good deal more regular as no great speed was reached. I enjoyed it as it was different, and that is what Rose wanted for me, something different, an escape from my thoughts. The one station I remember well, we stopped at for some time was called Login. Some trucks were shunted off the rear of the train and pulled by some horses into a siding. I had never seen such a thing before, even though I heard it was quite a regular occurrence. I was starting to relax. The little train chuffed into Cardigan station, just one platform and a goods shed. Alongside was a wide and crystal-clear river, so different to the coal dust carrying industrial rivers back home.

Once we had alighted Rose saw her friend waving madly at us. If there was ever a nondescript woman with hardly a redeeming feature it was Rose's friend, Margaret. Her age mid thirty's, her clothes drab and the shake of her hand limp. I think we both took an instant dislike to each other. That is all I want to say relative to Margaret.

There were horse cabs and carriages picking up the few passengers that there were. The atmosphere was so different to home that an unnatural smile came over my face. It was one of happiness but not knowing why. Even Weston and my rural boarding school did not ooze the pleasures of my first experience of Cardigan. Rose had telegrammed and booked me a room in the Lion Hotel, which I was informed by the dreary Margaret, was only a 10-minute walk away. They went off together in a cab after arrangements were made for them to call at the Lion for me in the morning. I tarried on the river bridge and watched the water pass beneath. There were many trading boats at the quay, nothing anywhere near the size of the ships back home. That was a real seaport, this was one of a gentler kind and less people. I reached the Lion easily, it being a straight walk. It was an hotel that fronted the main street, with a large canopy supported by two pillars, over the pavement. I entered my details in their register. The room were sufficient, high sprung beds with equally as high sprung mattress. The fire in the room had been set but no likelihood of being lit in the warm weather of Cardigan on that day. I went for a walk up the town's main street, the market hall had just closed but there were some traders dismantling their stalls, outside the hall in the street. I noticed the prices were reduced, especially the perishables, as there was no way they would have been fresh the following day. Some of the street shops still had doors open, and grocers, fruiterers and all were taking their display goods back indoors.

As I walked up one side of the street, my plan was to cross and walk down the other. It was a market town, and I was just experiencing the dying embers of the trading day. I stopped to investigate a tuck shop. There were humbugs in many shapes and sizes. If it had been open, I would have bought a quarter to share with Rose. I turned to resume my walk but on doing so I noticed two men walking towards me. They looked as their gait was effortless. They were wearing identical long grey coats with hoods. Their appearance caused me to stand motionless. Their heads were looking downwards, and those old feelings of fear and catastrophe started to engulf me. They were coming for me, they just would not leave me in peace. The sounds of the Cardigan day fell silent and my whole being crumpled. When they were a few yards away from me their heads gradually raised. It was Dad and Ron. They were beckoning me to come to them. A slow teasing movement of the fingers. I shook violently, there was nothing I could do to stop it. They had no eyes, just holes, no eyes. They smiled, as though perpetrating pleasure. In that terrible moment, I dropped to my knees, my head bowed. The shaking of my limbs was now so bad and my situation ridiculous, that I looked to the heavens and pleaded with the Lord to take me away from this hell. Above me the dead men started to beckon me up. I was aware of other people around me. I had been in this position before where I was the only one who could see these demons. I was being stared at by shoppers who were keeping their distance and shouting at me. I remember shouting back, 'Can't you see them? Can't you see them? They're dead. Help me please help me'. No-one did. I felt my tormentor's power as they spread their arms out enticing, appealing, nay demanding, me to rise up to them. 'I am not dead. I am not dead...' were the words I screamed. 'No, no, you cannot have me!'. I was then physically clutched by someone, who put his arm around my neck pulling me backwards. I could see Dad and Ron with their arms out, floating just above. They wanted me but I did not want them. My desire to get away suddenly brought power back to my limbs. A crowd was around me, and in that crowd I thought I had a glimpse of Rose. 'Rose, Rose, tell

Dad to go, tell him to go, please....' I remembered no more.

## CHAPTER TWENTY-TWO

I awoke in a small room. Once again, I was in some form of custody even though I had done nothing. There was a tight jacket strung around me which made movement impossible. The first thing my eyes made out was Rose with a policeman by her side. 'Rose, Rose', I blurted out, 'Dad and Ron were there. Rose it was horrible. Tell me you saw them, please tell me someone saw them'.

Rose smiled and shook her head, 'No Eli, I did not see them. No-one saw them. It was all in your mind'. She stood and spoke as though excited and enjoying my plight, and that annoyed me greatly.

The policeman spoke, 'Saw who? You are ill son, very ill. You cannot stay here in Cardigan. We are arranging an appearance before the local court for tomorrow.'

I interrupted, 'Did you see them?'

'No son, we saw nothing. Your lady friend here is arranging a telephone call to your mother to let her know. I am charging you with a common law Breach of the Peace in Cardigan. There are numerous witnesses to your behaviour'. He intimated to Rose to leave with him, she followed him out, but not before she turned around a grinned. Her behaviour was extraordinary. The gate slammed and there I was again, locked up and very much on my own.

Hours went by and my confusion reached new

levels. I was led into a tiny court room which was packed with people. The secure jacket I was wearing constricted movement to such an extent, I could only look the way I was being led. I was pushed to sit on a bench in the dock of the court. Either side, and in front, were men with pens and paper. It was a small court room, with an air of ruralism. One of the men, dressed in a fine dark suit, stood, turned and said, 'I am going to speak for you. I am going to ask for a remand until tomorrow so I can understand your position and put the facts before their Honours'. I nodded and almost immediately was pulled up to stand, as two  military looking men walked in and sat down, but not before bowing to the small assembly, all men. My court appearance was minimal. It was little more than a circus. I was asked no questions as it appears the picture painted of me was demonic, a mad man, a lunatic. I did manage to shout, 'My dead Dad was there....' But as soon as I opened my mouth a hand was put over it and I was dragged backwards and downwards into a cell once more.

I was accommodated in Cardigan police station, tied up like a madcap, and fed just rough white bread and water. My hands were not allowed free, and I was fed by the same policeman who had charged me with breach of the peace. Rose did not come to see me, I had heard nothing from mother, I was alone. In a few days, I lost count how many, a horse carriage took me, still tied, to the Cardigan railway station. I was in the protection of two men stated to be attendants at a Briton Ferry Asylum. My journey up this railway line only days before had been a pleasant one, a holiday excursion to escape the ills of my life and recover, in the pleasing company of Rose. I was returning a prisoner to a new home, an asylum for lunatics.

## CHAPTER TWENTY-THREE

I had a visitor. Two months locked in a room for most of the day and night with no-one to talk to, now I was told I was to have a visitor. The weeks that had passed had lessened the warders concern for me. The jacket was now permanently off, and I was, as one warder put it, 'just an ordinary bloke who had a bad day'. My obvious intelligence and common sense shone through. I was not like the others in that asylum, I am sure. That display in Cardigan had dissolved out of their minds, and mine too if I am to be honest, but now I was to have a visitor.

I went through names, Tom, Jeremiah, Patrick, Rose, mother, and of all of them, it was mother I wanted to see. I was to be walked by two warders to a secure visitor's box. My grandest feeling was that I was to be trusted to walk the corridors without the jacket on. I know I was much better, and everyone could see that. My mind's madness in seeing my deceased father and Ron, I put down as a temporary bout of insanity brought on by the absurd events of the past few years. My father's empty grave, the search for treasure, the séance, the shocking bouts in hospital all brought on incongruity in me. I was going to finish with it all, move away, move on in life. Bristol, Birmingham, London all were calling, or so I felt. I was going to tell my mother as soon as I saw her, and I sensed today was the day to do so. I could not wait to see her.

The questions in my head were endless, the first being, why it has taken so long for her visit me, or indeed anyone to visit. I know I shall soon be out, and with her assistance I can be pledged a good home, which the asylum Superintendent cannot refuse me surely. The courts would have to agree, but with a witness from the Superintendent, it should be a formality. I wondered how mother was. She had seemed so melancholy over the last few years, even her new pub, the Cottage, had not really cheered her. The shock of my father's empty grave would have brought bad luck and ill feeling on anyone, she though took it calmly. I was starting to think deeply again so I changed my focus to those days on the dray with Tom. The sylvan lanes, the wistful days of my early years, seemed easy to reproduce. A smile came over my face whenever I thought about them.

I heard the key turn in the lock of my room door. It swung open and there were the two warders who were to take me see my visitor. They were men of mature years, hardened by their work, but still with a sense of humour and humanity. They talked to me as if one of them. I was normal in their eyes now. 'Eli, time to go son. Off to see your visitor'.

'Who is it?' I enquired eagerly.

'A lady'.

# CHAPTER TWENTY-FOUR

The walk to the visitor's hall was pleasant although taking only a minute or so. The warders chatted between themselves, I could have heard every word, but I was too excited. I wanted to know whether my mother was well and did she feel bad of me. A feeling of shame had encompassed me recently, although I know I had done nothing to be ashamed of. The large double doors were opened by a warder, and we all entered. I was shown to a cubicle which was open on my side but enclosed for my mother. I noted some of the inmates had secure coats on, with warders at arm's length. I was left on my own. My two warders kept me in sight but sat back at a long table which was situated along the wall behind. There was an urn there, the attraction was obvious. I sat alone for around five minutes staring through the grill onto an empty chair, then there was activity. A warder on the other side pulled the chair back and through the grill I saw a woman sit down. It was not my mother, who was it? I did not recognise her until she removed her bonnet and I saw the black hair and the eyes. It was the eyes I had last seen in Windsor Place. Madame Ella had come to see me!

My disappointment was equalled by my curiosity. I stared and simply enquired in a voice, no more than a whisper, 'Madame Ella?'

Her reply was a smile, and pressing in towards the

grill she said, 'Please Eli, call me Ellen'. Her voice was gentle, her smile captivating and her eyes not blazing any more, just mesmerising me. The new Madame Ella was probably the most beautiful woman I had ever seen. The darkness of the séance, her theatrics of the session forgotten, and now I was to call her Ellen. I was silenced just by her presence. 'I found out where you were Eli, from your lady friend Rose'.

I interrupted, 'Rose is not my lady friend. At least not anymore. We are friends, that's all'. It was a childish first piece of conversation, but the truth had to be known about Rose and me.

'Where is my mother then? Why are you here?' My questions did not go unnoticed, but Ellen spoke of something else.

'Eli, we have not long. You have got to help'. She leant towards me which prompted me to pull back. I was frightened. What was she about to say? I just nodded 'yes' as though I was in control of my own actions, which I was not. I wanted to leave, but that entrancing face held me still. 'Eli, your father and I were good friends. He had come to see me when I was based in the waxworks building...'

I interrupted at that point having cleared my throat and taken a very deep breath. I wanted to stop her there. 'Where is my mother? Do you know?'

She ignored me as though time was of the essence, which in truth it was. 'I had met afterwards Tom,

Jeremiah and your father's brother, Patrick. They wanted me to contact the dead to find the grave of a scribe monk in the cathedral grounds and the location of vast wealth buried in the woods to the north. I was supposed to call on the deceased persons who were involved in both incidents to get information...'

I interrupted 'For the good lord's sake, no more. I don't want to hear any more'.

The warders moved towards me as they could see I was agitated. The visit was going to be closed.

Ellen stood. With a dominant voice she pleaded, 'Eli, you must listen, you must help your father.' She hurried off and spoke to the warder guard that had led her in. At that moment I discovered if you are a beautiful woman, you can melt the hearts of men, and you have the power to entrap them. She returned and asked to see me tomorrow, permission having just been granted. My warders led me away but not before I turned to her, smiled and nodded my head positively. Even though she was much older, I was infatuated.

I walked back to my room along the miserable, dispiriting corridor with my two warders marching behind. Their steel tipped boots creating a noise that resonated harshly against the shiny brick walls and bringing out whimpers and shouts from behind those hellish doors. So many men wanting something that the warders could not bring, freedom! I could not get Ellen's countenance out of my mind. The door clicking shut, locking me once more into my awful space, did not on this occasion feel so final. I was to see her eyes again tomorrow, I was going to have a beautiful woman ask questions of me, questions I could not probably answer. I would ask questions of her first. Dad and treasure, Dad and contacting the dead. I sat on the floor and leant against the wall, even though hardly any light, but for once it did not matter. I felt resolute that I was going to ask Ellen questions, before I answered hers. In my short but eventful life I had learnt only too often that if you look forward to something, then it always seems the hours pass slower. Even the evening meal did not taste too bad, the warder opening the door to pass it to me, rather than the usual trap. I noted on his brief visit that his usual question of asking how I was feeling had turned into two. His second line of questioning was, 'Well, aren't you going to tell us who she was? What did she want?' I did not even know the warder's name. That may appear surprising, but in all these months, I had never heard it. If I had I am sure I would have remembered it.

The night was long and sleep challenging. I hoped against hope that I was as sane as the next man, in fact I knew I was, my visitations were real as my clear reactions. Ellen was going to prove it once and for all. I had really encountered the dead!

## CHAPTER TWENTY-FIVE

There she was! Ellen, eyes burning, dressed in black, her bonnet now gone letting the silken black hair fall about her shoulders. She was waiting to talk to me, Eli McNamara! I sat, determined to listen and to say nothing, but I was in for a shock, and it was not long coming. Once again, the warders let us be, this on both sides of the freedom divides.

'Eli, please, please listen. I am only allowed 15 minutes as you know'. I nodded. 'You are a unique kind of person. You have joined your father and Ron in a singular group of people who are blessed with a power far beyond the normal. When you came to Windsor Place you left in the arms of the police and then to a secure hospital. You lost your mind, they said. You had not Eli. You, like your father and Ron, are living conduits between the quick and the dead. But you Eli are even more remarkable. You did not die like your father and Ron. The madding did not have you. You are a super link, you keep your soul, and it is your soul that fights your battles and refuses to die. Your father lost his battle, and his body was taken. Ron's body has been taken too, and there are reasons...' I stopped her. I stood. Ron's body has gone, it was simply too much for me. I had not understood at that point what she was saying. I knew that if any more was said then I may react, and with an exaggerated reaction would come my destiny, and that destiny would be to stay in that dreadful cell all my life. I had to be normal. I looked at her and said 'Goodbye. I do not wish to hear any more'. I turned and joined my warders, who left their teacups and took me back along the long corridors and into my cell. It was only when I sat did I realise what I had done. I had reacted and was consequently left with major questions unanswered. Stupid, stupid man! I had done it again, I even shouted out loud the word stupid, which I hoped no-one in authority had heard.

The hours spent in lonely incarceration were now inflated by my foolishness which made each minute of the day an hour, and each hour a day. The vittles' visits were no solace, as the platters were delivered within seconds, not even enough to say, 'Good Day to you'. The Doctor's check-ups were now few and far between, I regarded myself, and I am sure they did, as a model patient. I had not hurt anyone whilst going through my troubles and was impatient for sweet release. My mother still had not come to see me. It had been a month or so since the visits of Ellen, and during those weeks, I found it hard to get her off my mind. A young man infatuated with an older woman is not easy, especially as there was, is, and can never be any future in such a liaison.

## CHAPTER TWENTY-SIX

I had been going to the chapel within the institution for many months, and Sundays was a day to look forward to. They usually sent one warder to fetch me, and he always stood adjacent in the little asylum chapel. It seated around twenty people and had a small, yet ornate, altar at the head of the nave area. The four benches either side of the aisle were basic in the extreme. The only colour to be seen was provided by some flowers in a jug placed on the altar table. My warder was a religious man and sung at the top of his tenor voice which covered up my squeaks and pathetic attempts to stay in tune to the harmonium. I was walked back to my room, the door slammed, and the hatch shut tight. My next caller would be my supper snack and then silence until the following morning. I say silence, but in truth it was often broken by the wails of some of the more witless patients incarcerated around me. It was a sad and unforgiving place.

The night was long, but the morning brought the most astounding of news and subsequent events. I was taken out of my room and walked to an office. My guard lit his pipe and sat on a chair next to me. He shrugged and said, 'Don't ask me, I don't know why we're here. I just does as I am told'. It reminded me of something Jeremiah had told me about rank structure within organisations, he then being a member of the constabulary. He told me the men at the top are secretive. They plot and plan, keeping the majority below them in the dark, until one day they pounce, causing havoc! My guard obviously knew nothing, nor it seems, was he interested anyway.

It was such an odd experience for me to be in an office first thing in the morning. I knew deep inside that the reason must be positive, and I was certainly correct in that supposition! Another warder, red of the face, and whiskered, who I had never seen before, came in and placed clothes upon my lap and said, 'Here you are, try these on'. They were outdoor clothes. I stripped off my shirt and leggings and tried the clothes on. It would not have mattered if they were too small, too big, too anything, I would not have complained. I was going somewhere. The ruddy faced man scooped up my rejects and left the room, pulling the door behind him with massive force, causing a bang, which made my pipe smoking, and sleepy personal guard, jump up and look around as though he had been shot. The door opened once more and this time it was the assistant Superintendent who marched in. He was dressed in the manner of a 'gentleman' and had a fine swagger and behind him was no other than Ellen. The surprises came fast for me on that day. Behind Ellen was none other than Jeremiah, still sporting his specious dog collar.

Ellen came across to me and with a purposeful hug she said, 'Eli you are coming with us. Father Jeremiah and I have come to take you home'. There would be no purpose in recording my thoughts at that moment as, to tell the world the truth, I had not the foggiest of ideas what was going on. I was led out of the room to the reception vestibule of the asylum where I signed a large book, then a ledger.

The warder on reception, a rather diminutive and bespectacled gentleman, turned to me and said, 'Goodbye Eli. You have done well here. You are free to go with your guardians. A warning though, even though the magistrates and the superintendent have signed you off into the care of your loving friends, you must report to a medical doctor in the first week. On this you are to be accompanied by one or other of your guardians. Do you understand?' I nodded.

Jeremiah interjected, 'He is in safe hands now. Ellen and I will care for his every need'. With that, I was walked out to a waiting fly and off to the local railway station for my journey home.

The explanation for the peculiar occurrences of that morning was soon forthcoming. The fly reached the station, my two saviours and I alighted, and I walked alone and free onto the platform. Jeremiah and Ellen watched as I walked up and down the platform breathing in the liberty of a free man. They looked a fine couple. The tall, strong and imposing Jeremiah, standing alongside the compelling and delightful Ellen. I would have been proud to have called them father and mother at that moment, in that place, all those years ago.

The thought though was dispelled with some

haste, and glad I am for it. Ellen told me not to ask questions until we were on the train, and Jeremiah, who was getting numerous marks of respect from fellow passengers and railway staff alike, just nodded his head slowly in agreement. A porter bowed his head as he passed Jeremiah and said, 'Morning Father', to which Jeremiah replied, 'Bless you and the day ahead'. I knew it was a charade. I knew he was not really a man of God, but I had been away a long time, perhaps times had indeed changed. I was to find out they had not!

The train ride was undertaken in a compartment with others; therefore, questions of depth were difficult, but I ascertained I was going to be taken to Tom's house in Scott Street. It was where I was to reside for the projected future. Each time I was about to burst with a question a quick nod of the head from Father Jeremiah indicated 'not now'. We were met at the General station by two more friends, Tom and Patrick, but not my mother! The walk to Tom's small house took no more than five minutes. I was now fully cognisant of everything around me, the people, the noises, the location, the atmosphere and the freedom. I was the true Eli McNamara once more. We all squeezed into Tom's parlour. Patrick took the gently simmering black iron kettle from the hearth-stand in preparation for a drink. I noticed Ellen did not even offer to assist. She acted as though a lady of fine breeding, who would have been used to a maid.

My newfound confidence spurred me on to stand and demand answers. I was no child anymore. My breakdown in Cardigan was nothing more than that, a breakdown. My father was dead, then I remembered the empty grave and my spirited confidence diminished a little.

My day in the parlour of that little house in Scott Street was one of revelation after revelation. All were present, my father's brother Patrick, Jeremiah, Tom and Ellen. To attempt to relive the conversational process and the whys and wherefores would be impossible, therefore I will summarise the infinitely disturbing tale, but start with the most devastating and repulsive piece of information I believe I had ever heard. Ron was my half-brother! My school chum, my close friend was purportedly my brother. It was told at the very commencement of the meeting, and it obviously caused me so much distress that Ellen crossed and hugged me close to her. It was Patrick who spoke of Ron's mother, a single woman who brought up Ron as her own. My Dad, and known to no-one, assisted with the finances and concerns of the woman. Ron was apparently ignorant as to the fact I was his half-brother. Then why tell me? This fell to Ellen who brought a small stool and sat directly in front of me. Everything slowly slipped into place as Ellen spoke. It was a blunt and uncompromising recent history of the McNamara family.

Dad had gone to see Madame Ella, as he called her

then. She was in great demand to reach out to other realms, and to other persons long dead. It was his belief that Ellen could help him in a quest so improbable that it would have caused many a stir even in London circles. She persuaded him, with good reason, that she could indeed communicate with persons long dead, and on many an occasion this was done. Ellen stated to me that my father was the most sensitive and vibrant of men she had ever dealt with. His intensity and sensory element were unique. Whosoever they attempted to reach out to, caused a sensation between them. They were bonded together, one worked with the other to bring back the long dead who spoke to them. Their spirits, their souls were linked. Ellen and he were mouthpiece agents to the reincarnated dead. One could not work without the other. My father became obsessed, not only with his newfound abilities to reach out to the past, but with Ellen. I remember quite clearly on hearing this, the distancing between my mother and father. Perhaps she knew.

Ellen continued with the upsetting narrative. It was found that Ron had the same power to communicate. How they found out was not conveyed to me, but there was a downside to all this. On each occasion of communication there was a great demand on Dad's and Ron's mind. It was as though they were being invaded. Ellen, fascinated by the synergy between the three of them, persuaded Patrick to come over from Wexford in

Ireland. It was found he did not have the psychic power of Ron and Dad. This proved that it was Dad's line that held the power. I was of Dad's line and my recent hallucinations were not hallucinations at all. I had come face to face with the dead! I remembered Ron's terror in the old castle on the hill and the tumbling chase away and across the fields. They were both dead now. I was the next! That meeting in the parlour had one more shock for me. I was informed that my darling Rose was part of the conspiracy to get me to the séance. How could she have done that? I felt betrayed. I remember rising and walking out of the front door and away.

No-one attempted to physically stop me except Jeremiah who called, 'Eli, you have to stay in this house or you will be retaken back to the asylum'. I listened but ignored. My intention was to get to the Cottage pub to see my mother. She was the only one I believed was left lucid among us. She had been wronged and needed my sympathy.

The walk through town was strange, freedom was odd. I had borrowed some of Tom's clothes and was unused to that appearance. My path took me close by the yard of my employers. I could smell the brewery and imagine everyone working within. I walked past the Red Lion and thought of Ron and the conversation. He had passed on, yet I was informed his body was missing, a duplication of my father's disappearance.    It was a half hour later that I reached the Cottage pub. It stood where two small, terraced streets met and was the main building on the corner. It was shut. Out of the first-floor window was sticking a sign notifying people that it was for sale. I crossed the road and spoke to the man and woman on their doorstep opposite. My enquiry ascertained that my mother had left some weeks ago and gone 'up country' to reside near her son. They did not know where. My life was going from bad to worse and I knew that the only place I could go now was Scott Street and the little front bedroom of Tom's terraced house. It was not a good situation for anyone to be in, it was going to get a good deal graver. I meandered my way back to Scott Street to find that it was only Tom within. This was a great relief as I did not feel threatened by him, and I knew him well, much better than the others. Tom had been my friend since my early childhood in the Royal and for that I had always been thankful. I had been given five shillings from the poor box at the asylum and I used four pence of it to buy a loaf of white bread. I need not have bothered. Tom had prepared a dinner of meat and potatoes with a pitcher of ale to wash it down afterwards.

## CHAPTER TWENTY-SEVEN

What followed over the next few months was nothing more than cruelty, and I was on the receiving end of it. I had been rescued from the dreadful torment of the asylum, only to find it was not kindness, but greed, that was behind it. I was unique, I was the key to a fortune. I was introduced to a new style of acquaintance, which even Tom was mindful of, the acquaintance of obsession. I was told time and time again that my father would have wanted me to help them. After all, they were all members of his group.

The reality of my position had pushed me into a corner, and it was a dark one. I was kept in food by Tom, kept in accommodation by Tom and kept out of the asylum by Tom. The family I had known were gone, all driven out by Dad's obsession with the dead and riches. I was informed that I was to be taken out on a night duty and Ellen would be in charge. A meeting had been arranged and Tom told me in no uncertain terms that I was to participate, as it may be my own fathers last chance to rest in peace.

I sat in an armchair in Tom's front room, alone for now, knowing that in a couple of hours the little space would be full of the foolish, as I called them. It was they, who should be in an asylum. Tom, Jeremiah, Patrick, the beautiful, but deceitful Ellen and Rose. Their lives had been wounded by séance and visitations. The confusion I was engulfed in was dark, and to become darker. Obsession and avarice had eliminated decency.

The time came and they arrived and packed the little room. The only one missing was Madame Ella, the sly Ellen. It was the power of her looks, her charisma, her confidence, that fascinated us all. She arrived a few minutes late, which was unusual. Dressed all in black, she swept in, or at least attempted it. She had to shuffle to gain a position of power within the room, which ultimately meant standing up against the door, which she had closed behind her.

Let me summarise the next hour of conversation into a few pertinent sentences. Ellen wanted me to go to the Cathedral graveyard at dusk and contact the dead. The dead being my father and Ron. She said she had been bombarded with knowledge within her weekly seances. She had been told the last resting place of the 12th century monk, Geoffrey of Monmouth, and it was me who would see the manifestation. No-one asked her where the knowledge had come from. Something inside me was telling me to run and keep running, start a new life a long way from this town. There were alternatives though. Do what was asked of me and face up to my demons in the shape of my father and Ron or, face being dispatched back to the asylum. I was in their hands.

I agreed to the scenario they all wanted, attend a séance in the graveyard. Only Rose would not be there, a truth of which I was very pleased indeed. Her small part in the conspiracy was done and everyone was aware that she annoyed me.

## CHAPTER TWENTY-EIGHT

We gently made our way down the Bishop's Steps that led to the base of the cathedral tower. It had been raining and the steps were slippery. The raindrops still dripped from the leaves of the high bushes and trees that guarded either side of that long stepway. It was Ellen who led the way, I followed, and behind were Tom, Patrick and Jeremiah. One long line of anxious, nervous, and hesitant people. Ellen entered the graveyard to the right of the main entrance and tower. Dusk had taken its toll on my thoughts; the day seeming more dependable. Jeremiah's assurances that the western graveyard area was always quiet at this time, was proved correct. We were the only people present. His appearance of a man of holy orders would surely have reassured any locals wondering of what we were about. The loneliness of my situation though, surely was apparent to all. They were going to see nothing. It was my reaction and narrative that would enthuse everyone and yet, even knowing I would not be laughed at, or put into some asylum; I was still fearful. To come face to face with my dead father, my dead friend, nay brother, was a scenario surely no-one had experienced before. Our well-practised routine would clearly mean nothing now. The three men moved away and leant against a wall leaving Ellen and I together. Ellen stood, dressed totally in black, her hair melting into her clothes.

145

I imagined her eyes on fire and ready to take on humankind. 'If there is anyone here Eli they will come to you. Stay calm'. The truth is I was not calm. How could I be? I was feeling cold, a tingling down my back. I had seen how Ron had originally reacted, his fright, his run for his life. His madding!

I believed Ellen that the only danger in apparitions was the fright we ourselves perceived, and there was no need for fright. They would not harm me. The only noises now heard were the distant banging of doors in the dwellings not too far away. An owl screeched, just once, and was gone, which added to the power of the moment. The stillness adorned the cold and menacing earth. They seemed in union.

Ellen's long, majestic cloak brushed the undergrowth as she moved into a position near me. The tombstones stood silent sentinel to portraits of the past, the priest's tone, the sobbing of the women, the whimpering of the children and the stern faces of men. Some stones had fallen, some hugged by ivy, some big, some small, all with stories to reveal. Ellen started to sing, albeit an unrecognisable tune, and my nerves reacted by bringing me well and truly out of my dreaming into stark reality. Dusk had turned into night, letting the sky illuminate the nooks and crannies of the cathedral graveyard. Ellen's singing was gentle, it was a hymn of some sort. I heard the name Lord God on a few occasions. The men behind me, the 'Treasure Hunters', only wanted money, it was me who had to face demons, and one was my father!

Ellen continued her hymn. The stage was set in that most grim of places. 'Sing with me Eli' she ordered. 'Sing any hymn to the Lord'.

I did as I was told and began to sing a hymn taught me by Bertha in the basement of the Royal, all those years ago. 'Rock of Ages, cleft for me, let me hide myself in thee. Let the water and the blood, from thy riven side which flowed, be of sin the double cure, cleanse me from its guilt and power'. I only remembered the first verse and I kept repeating it. With each repetition my singing got louder, as with it, my confidence. Ellen had moved to stand alongside of me, and I heard her voice, muted low, joining me in song. In truth, I felt foolish, nay stupid, yet if Ellen was the intermediary and I was one of the advocates it had to be done. Tonight, the atmosphere was different to the others. I felt odd, I felt humbled, I felt intense. I felt a sense of power within me, as truly it was. The stiffening up of my body sent trembles down my shoulders through my arms which made my whole being tense. Ellen had stopped singing and my voice had diminished to nothing more than a murmur. This was it! I knew this was it. The madding of Eli McNamara.

Was I to join father and Ron in that awful remoteness between life and death? I did not want to die, I wanted to live. I knew I had seen death. Ellen and the rest knew as well, the oddity and greediness of human nature knew no bounds. The time had come. There in the distance across the graveyard I saw light. I heard leaves start to murmur having been brought to life by a breeze. There was no reaction from Ellen.

The sound I made was one that may have emanated from an innocent baby, a kind of whimper. Having prior knowledge of the living dead is no panacea to dread. I sensed Ellen sidle away and disappear. She was leaving me on my own. I could not turn, or look left or right, my eyes were fastened onto two figures approaching. These were not figures of normal human bodily movement. There was no scrambling between gravestones, or over cumbersome lumps, they seemed to be gliding towards me. This was it, Dad and Ron had come to claim me, but I was aware this time I was untouchable, I was not a lunatic, an asylum case. I was a living, breathing human being and they could not touch me. Frighten me yes, but apparitions cannot kill. Ellen and the men had schooled me well.

I shouted out 'Lord, Lord protect me', as Ellen had told me. The phantoms came nearer and when around ten yards distance from me, stopped. Their long grey coats and hoods looked somehow theatrical, yet there was no drama in the reality of my situation, it was actual! Dad's face had those awful black eye holes, as did Ron's. The shaking in my arms became so forceful that soon my whole being replicated it. I had no control over any part of my body. The muscles in my buttocks relaxed and I felt warmth in my breeches, an experience not known before to me. In truth I was terrified. That dreadful moment in Cardigan when I saw the apparitions come toward me, did not match the setting of this night. A graveyard, dark with an unholy breeze blowing and bending its way among the tombstones. The smiles over the grey faces of my father and brother, indicated something. What that something was, at that very time, I did not know. I shouted out at the top of my voice for help, but I knew it would not be forthcoming. I tried and tried again to make a noise to indicate to Ellen that I was not alone anymore. Where were they all? Safely away from harm, letting me face the wrath of the half dead. Noise was building up all around the graveyard. The tree branches now bending and the flowers, many long dead, were being blown out of their funeral containers and towards me. The detritus of a graveyard coming alive in the night wind.

Then stillness; nothing. The graveyard and its surrounds became silent. I noted Dad and Ron separate, this near the ancient, sculptured doorway and along the cathedral wall. The silence continued. I commenced to walk slowly into the scene, towards Dad. I had no control at all and was numbed why I should be doing this. The smiles on their faces were wicked. They were dead, I kept repeating they were dead and I was alive. I walked deeper into the graveyard and into a position facing the wall. They had their backs to the wall and about two feet from it. They were staring at me. A blurred light came from somewhere, with probability the night sky, yet I could not look up to see. It then happened, something that threw me once again into sheer horror, but this time barely describable. The ground started to rumble as if in earthquake. Between the two apparitions, and gradually from the ground, emerged a hooded head. Its stare was directly at me. Then the shoulders appeared, and slowly more of a body came out of the ground. Now a trio of the dead. I was desperately holding on to the thought that God would protect me. Here they were, Dad, Ron and the spectre of a monk, the hood creating a dark shadow over the face area. The monk moved his head back and the hood fell. He too had no eyes, just black holes. He was bald and his face was skeletal covered by yellow skin, what was left of it, as it wrapped around his facial bones. He was carrying a jar, a large one, the size perhaps of a jeroboam. The monk lifted it high above his head, then brought it down, aiming it towards me. My scream had no power and no worth. Without warning the three apparitions pushed forward, proclaiming their evil intent to possess me. My voice finally overcame my fright and I screamed out, 'Help me, for God's sake help me!' I threw myself to the ground, attempting to dig with my bare hands into the earth to escape. I pressed my face into it, as though in need of my own grave. It was madness, the concept of a lunatic. I felt a strong hand pull at me, there were shouts and cries. The monk had me! The only escape was to run, yet my body craved to be close to the earth.

It was Jeremiah who had gripped me around the chest and was pulling me away. Ellen yelled, 'What do you see Eli, what do you see?' She was flung away by Tom who then joined Jeremiah in pulling me from graveyard and onto the flat area of the cathedral entrance. My screams resounded against the giant door and must have been heard across the village. Patrick put his hand over my mouth. I was now in a similar state of mind as Cardigan. This time I would not be arrested and locked away in a lunatic asylum. I was with friends.

I was aware of other people approaching nearby. Young lovers perhaps kernoodling in the darkness of the cathedral's byways, rudely shaken out of their ecstatic state by my screams. I stopped and simply lay there breathing heavily and thanking the Lord that I had friends around me for protection. I was not going back to an asylum, it was that simple fact that kept me aware of circumstances. My education by Ellen assisted also. They could see nothing, other than my reactions to those awful creatures. I was propped against the cathedral door and forced, and that was the word, 'forced', to take whisky from a bottle that Patrick had produced from his great coat pocket. My rescuers wanted me to relay my experience right then and there. I was not ready to do it. I needed time to myself to understand and absorb what I had just seen.

More curious people joined others to stare at me.

Jeremiah, in his most regal of voices, told everyone that a fit had befallen me. There was nothing to worry about and he was in charge. Many drifted off, some hand in hand, to renew their spooning. I asked to be taken to Tom's house and be left alone in bed. I just wanted to sleep my thoughts away.

## CHAPTER TWENTY-NINE

The short descent of those bare wooden stairs in Scott Street was more like a ladder into a nightmare. There were four persons keenly awaiting me to relive the occurrences of last evening, none of it for my wellbeing, but all for their gain. I had woken thinking why not leave Dad and Ron to their eternal rest? The world they had descended into, between life and death, was a punishment from the devil. They did not deserve it. Let them go.

That tiny front room had five chairs placed around the fine, yet modest, dinner table. I was greeted as if a celebrity straight off the Hippodrome's stage, and not from the humble bedroom just above. I knew what I had seen in the cathedral graveyard, the four present had not! I had been through the most terrifying experience. Could there be anything worse, than seeing your dead father?

Ellen welcomed me as though I was a celebrity, a long-lost relative. The excitement was palpable. Sitting around the table I started to speak but was consistently interrupted with questions. Jeremiah appeared to be the controller of the inquisition and for that I was grateful. I went over everything I had seen, which brought glances and words of astonishment from my little audience. The most potent of responses came when I told of the monk figure appearing out of the ground. Ellen's mouth opened as though she was in some sort of shock, which I presumed she was. She looked at the others, who were all shaking their heads in disbelief. I told them he was a little shorter than Dad and Ron but a deal stockier. I remembered the remnant of a white beard was evident on his face, his pallid skin just about clinging on to a face with holes where the eyes should have been. I kept telling them that I was terrified and could not note everything. They could not possibly comprehend the horrifying vision and its effect on me, so it must have been a bizarre spectacle to see me hideously reacting to nothing. The most important piece of evidence I gave, which caused a heady reaction from all, was the mention of the jar. I was asked to describe the jar, its size, its colour, its condition and what the monk did with it. I explained that the most horrifying of the experience was when he came towards me, as if offering the jar. It was then I had thrown myself to the ground in terror.

Jeremiah stood up and pressed his arms on the table. 'Stop, that's enough', he exclaimed. 'No more. Eli is fatigued in the extreme'. I was grateful. Tom poured me a beer from a pitcher which had been placed on the windowsill. It was the best beer at the best time. There was an excitement in the room, the like of which I had not experienced before. Tom, Jeremiah, Patrick and Ellen were enthused, their conversation had an excited chatter. I left to wash myself in the back scullery, the stone sink big enough to allow me to lower my head into the cold water. I did this several times before shaking and rubbing my hair with a thick towel that hung behind the pantry door. I went back and joined the others. Their enthusiasm to discuss had diminished. It was Jeremiah who informed me of the culmination of their discussion, the lost grave of Geoffrey of Monmouth.

It was Patrick who spoke in representation of the others. 'Eli, do you remember you were given the book 'Mort D'Arthur' to read?'. I nodded. 'Do you remember within those pages the stories, heavily embellished, but having the same theme as a thread running through them, the life of King Arthur of the Britons. The magic of Merlin and the visits to the shores of Britain by Joseph of Arimathea, magical stories from the mists of time'. He kept his stare on me as he picked up a small pitcher of beer which he consumed in one swallow.

I had the time to ask one question. 'And this book is the reason Dad was in the cathedral yard?'

'Your father,' answered Jeremiah, 'knew of the story of the monk and author Geoffrey of Monmouth being buried in the confines of the cathedral or at least nearby. It was Geoffrey who brought Arthur and Merlin to the notice of peoples around the world as a fighter for good. The stories are simply unbelievable, yet they have been embroidered and proliferated to such an extent, the legends have turned to reality'.

Patrick interrupted, 'And it was said that Geoffrey got all his knowledge from lost manuscripts and books of the dark ages in Britain. He wrote numerous books extolling the virtues of the great Christian King Arthur. We believe he was also the man who wrote the Book of Llandaff in the 1140s'. This book tells of other major happenings, yet none can be verified'.

I could see Tom and Ellen eager to speak and enter the excitement of the moment.

I had had enough. 'For Heaven's sake, can't one of you just tell me what I was doing in that graveyard?' I had shouted the words. Everyone sat except Patrick.

'Eli, that man you saw we believe was none other than Geoffrey, the monk. He had risen from his grave, alongside your father and your brother, to show the jug that is still within. Inside that jug are items too valuable to comprehend. We must dig it up. That is the reason you were there. Your father has triumphed. Now we want you to find the Spanish treasure in the woods'. My reaction was a laugh, a laugh that did not go down well. They were beyond obsessional.

Ellen spoke. I stared at her and knew I was going to believe every word she uttered. 'You Eli are unique. You should be dead, yet you are not. I have never been so taken with anyone or anything in my life as I am with you. You have bridged the gap between life and death and fallen on the side of the living. Your father and Ron, fell on the side of the dead. Their presence will be gone soon when they realise you are not going to join them, therefore they are doing everything they can to pull you in'. She was on fire, I could almost feel her beauty, let alone see it.

Tom continued, 'And you must finish what has been started. Your conduit, Ellen, is going to the northern woods. Just one more interaction and you will be free Eli, free to enjoy the plunder, just as your father wanted. He wants us, and especially he wants you, to be rich Eli'. Each head was staring at me intently. Magnificent Ellen was transfixed but I knew it was the strange powers within me that attracted her and not Eli McNamara the man.

'Excuse me everyone, I want fresh air and to be on my own. I feel the head on these shoulders is too young to carry so much responsibility'. I took hold of my coat and walked out into Scott Street and the real world.

## CHAPTER THIRTY

I did not feel as I should. I felt detached from all those around me and was becoming single minded in my desire to go somewhere else, but where? I had lost trust in everyone. Mother, Rose, Tom, Jeremiah, there was no-one now I could trust. My brothers and sisters had been ushered out into other parts of the country, where I did not know. I could not grieve at my father's grave even if I had wanted to. He had deceived me more than any of the others. Those tranquil days of my past were a lie, all around me conspirators running agendas. I caught sight of my employer's brewery and I knew things would never ever be the same again. I could no more have entered that place than I could have sprouted wings and flew. Everyone I had ever known thought me insane. I was not going back to Scott Street. I did not want to see any of my so-called friends and family again. I had no money in my pocket and knew of no-one I could ask. I was not willingly going through that hell again. I kept saying to myself, 'No more, no more'. A new identity, a new path in life, hundreds of miles away from Ellen and Jeremiah. I planned to grow a beard, what need I of a razor? A new life, a new man, a new job.

My wandering took me up to the canal side at North Road. There were barges heading south to the docklands and north to the industrial coalfields. A strange feeling came over me, I could fall in and let the water do the rest. I was confused and lightheaded. No human being should go through what I had. I kept opening and closing my eyes to clear my mind. I was walking too fast; my speed was increasing compared to other people walking the same path. I was out of control and had no longer any understanding of my direction. I tried to shout to a man steering his horse on the canal path. I could see him, but he was gone in an instance. Nobody was taking any notice of me as I moved at a frantic pace. I remember thinking 'Is this what death is? Is my body in the canal and my soul racing to heaven'. I was careering towards somewhere. Where that somewhere was, I did not know. There was a castle, but it was gone within a blink of the eye. I was in a forest and standing among pine trees, and very much alone. I had regained use of my capacities and bent down to scoop up earth to prove it was reality; it was! I was breathing air heavily through my nose. I pinched it with my thumb and forefinger of my right hand. It hurt; I was alive.

What had happened in the last few minutes I could not, and did not want to understand. I was about to enter another chapter of my short life, which I thought may have been my final. The earth around four yards in front of me started to create a mound, just like I had seen moles do in Jeremiah's Garden. Three mounds were gradually becoming bigger, the earth and grasses falling to the sides. I held onto one thought. Nothing dead can hurt me. Out of the three mounds simultaneously rose figures in large shroud cloaks.

'Oh my God, not again, please not again. I cannot take any more'. No-one listened, not even the good Lord. On this occasion the figures grew and grew in height until they were towering over me and staring down. Their heads moved gently up and down in unison, the deep eye holes in their faces were vile. I backed away even though the shock of the evil dead was being diminished with each reawakening, I was in horror. I screamed 'Dad, why are you doing this to me?'

Screams were futile. I sat down with my legs crossed staring at the souls of my father and brother. I was accepting of the madding. I was unsure of the third ghoul; he was the middle of the three and kept beckoning me towards him with a slow movement of the hand. Death was calling! There was no noise other than the breeze and my intense breathing. My screams had gone, my voice had been silenced. I had no fear as I sat there awaiting my fate, the culmination of my life. Then, after a lifetime of seconds, the apparitions gradually began sinking into the earth, the mounds gone; it was as though it had never happened. There had been no Ellen to initiate them, there was no witnesses to note my actions or hear my cries. It came to me at that moment of silence what I had just seen.

Dad and the men had been tracing treasures in two

places, the cathedral graveyard and the woods to the north. Dad had found them and now it was me who had to tell the  group what I had seen. How did I get here? If I had just witnessed the reincarnation of Father I could not be dead! Ridiculous comment, but that is how I felt. I had fallen once more in the parallel between the two worlds. Something, or someone, had prevented me from passing over to the other side. I went to a fir tree where the mounds of earth had been. I broke off a small branch, then pushed it into the ground as a marker. I pushed it deep. I turned around and around noting the location. Within all the turmoil I could still operate as Elijah Llewellyn McNamara, in the realm of the quick.

My Good Lord, thank you. I have survived. The power of the occasion, the smell of the forest, the odious experience had pushed me from fight to flight. That flight was to see my legs ignore brambles, bushes, branches as I made that headlong dash back in the direction of town. Why I wanted to run I did not know, but run I did. The speed was above normality; I was not in control. I reached a village situated below a castle, which was swamped in a kind of unnatural haze, a whiteness across the sky yet mists at ground level. I was navigated into a public house; the sign carried its name, yet it was illegible to me. I did not want to go in there, I had not planned to be there, and I did not want to see anyone. The cavernous saloon was full. I stood, not knowing where I was or why I was there. The chattering slowly ceased, and every head turned towards me, then as one, looked down. Normal people in normal clothes. Some tall, some small, some with hats, some without. Men and women all looking to the planked and grubby floor, all in perfect calm. It was as if composed for a Greek tragedy. I tried to move out of it but could not.

Sitting on a bench, an old woman raised her head. It was Bertha. There was an appeal to her face, a sadness. Her glory days were over. I had always seen love in her look, now there was a sorrow. There was nothing on the table in front of her and either side of her were two old men both looking downwards. I was captivated by Bertha, the intimidation of the silence of the others was unimportant. She gradually smiled and moved her head up and down as though intimating a sort of yes. The two men commenced to copy her. I recognised them as two regulars at the Royal, regulars I knew were dead!

All around the room people stared and smiled, then moved their heads up and down in accord as if replicating life. Among them were no other than Dad and Ron. This was the ultimate confirmation that all the assembled company were dead! The souls of the travellers making their way into a new world, the world that is waiting for all of us. Bottles and glasses on the shelves began to move and rattle. Bertha slowly stood up. I witnessed her distinctive features ostensibly adjusting, as she looked around at the scores of faces packed into that room, all with their heads moving up and down, as if nodding yes. She walked towards me, and with that, every one of the other persons rose and made to move also. Their grins were consistent, their heads now still. I knew I had to make for Dad to help me out this hell. I rushed at him passing straight through the crowd. I had trusted Dad, I bloody trusted Dad and here he was again torturing me. There was confusion and, in the melee, screams, then fighting, punching and kicking.

I was thrown to the ground and felt the weight of people sitting on me, pulling at my arms and lying across my legs. I wanted to get to my despicable father, but how the hell do you destroy a dead man? The last thing I remember of that place was being prostrate on the floor with the sounds of panic and feeling punches and kicks about my body.

## CHAPTER THIRTY-ONE

I recall waking in a cell, still shouting and screaming, being held and having needles thrust into my arms. The nightmare was complete. It was a simple room with just an inspection hatch above ground level, and a palliasse on the flagged floor. The walls were not stone. I reached out to touch. It was a kind of padding. The hatch opened. A sallow, yet hardened face of a man looked through at me. He posted a document then slammed it shut.

I crawled to retrieve the paper. I leant my back against the soft wall and let the light from the small wind hole shine on it. It was predominantly a printed document but there were some handwritten notes thereon. I was charged with Assault, Damage, Breach of the Peace and several other acts of bad behaviour aimed at people I had no knowledge of. I saw it was addressed to me, Elijah McNamara. I took time to reflect before turning the document over. On the rear it stated in a copper plate handwriting. 'Found Guilty but Insane'. The Trial of Lunatics Act 1883.

I was a madman. I stood up and screamed, 'I am not a madman! I am not a madman!' I attacked the door pleading to be let out. The padding made no noise as I punched it. My screams and wails, it appeared, were beyond my control, no-one would listen. Where was Tom? His witness could release me.

How long I screamed for on that awful day I do not remember now. The madding had me. The job done. My insanity complete.

## CHAPTER THIRTY-TWO

It seems the loneliness of my room has taken away any knowledge I have of days, months or even years. The routine is just that, a routine. Each day I am led away to clear my own waste, always by three men. That is my exercise. I have just one arm free. When I arrive back at my room there is always a wooden platter of food placed in the middle of the floor. I am pushed in and the door slams shut.

Occasionally I am taken, marched, whilst securely held to a medical man's room. I am asked the same question. 'Have you seen any ghosts lately?' I can hear laughter. They expect my answer, it is always the same.

'Speak to Ellen, Jeremiah, Uncle Patrick, Rose or Tom, please speak to them. They will explain everything to you. I am not mad'. The reaction from the medical man to my plea is always to tick a piece of paper on the desk in front of him. I am then pulled away and marched to my room.

Time has brought an approach of a gentler nature from warders. I had ceased my caterwauling and once again in acceptance of my lot. My head hurt less, therefore I complained less. I noted how this had initiated the usual sense of empathy with my captors and kind-hearted questions were being asked of me on their daily visits, there being silence before.

I can write this down as a witness to my life,

because of a kindness. The medical man, on one of my visits, asked a different question. 'Is there anything you want? Anything that may help you pass the time?'

My reaction to that question took some time coming. 'Yes, paper and pencils. I want to write'.

He nodded, and with the first smile I had ever seen emanate from his face, he replied, 'You will get your paper and pencils Eli Llewellyn McNamara. Use them wisely'.

My life changed. I changed.

As you can see, I write during as many hours that I get light. Because of my timid behaviour, pencils and paper were always available. I still could not understand why no-one had come to visit me. None of my family, my friends, my associates, had written or even enquired as to my health, or given the authorities the explanations for my volatile behaviour.

To put into words that describe accurately the following experience would be even impossible for the great writers, such as Shakespeare and Dickens. I will give it the best of my efforts for you to comprehend the spectacle that occurred one late evening in my room.

I had been remembering and writing for the whole day, and I was exhausted. The only words spoken by me had been 'Thankyou'. That was my usual civility on the delivery of food platters. It must have been very late. The cries and screams of the unfortunates in adjoining rooms had diminished somewhat with fatigue. The night would probably be, as usual, punctuated by the occasional howl of the anguished.

My head was starting to hurt, and I felt dizzy. It was a frightful feeling and I remember shaking my head to clear it. The medication that had recently being forced in me by the men in white jackets was new, and I was informed it put me into some permanent state of torpor. I was a vegetable to be watered once a day and left to stagnate. Its worth was negligible as my writing, as you see, has prospered.

I was made aware of something behind me, I cannot say how I was made aware, I just was. I turned and saw a figure with its back against the door. It was inside the cell, yet the door had not opened. My head was starting to hurt as I had felt on many times before. I whispered, 'Please, please not again'. I shook my head violently to clear it and to remove the dark figure out of my imagination. The shaking, then screaming, did not work. It made the current visitation explosive. I dropped to my knees as my legs gave way, the fright causing me to involuntarily shake. I could not control it. The figure was clothed in the manner I had seen before, the face I had seen before, my craven father. He had come once more to steal my soul. I had thought I had seen the last of him, but it was not to be. There was not a movement, the gape, if I can call it that, emanating from the eye sockets, or where the eyes should be. I made no sound, unsure as to whether I could anyway. The hood on the figure's cloak gradually, with no assistance, moved back. The hair was long, grey, thick and tousled, the very antithesis of the neatness of my father when he was young and vibrant. This time he was different, aged in death. I was seeing my father in old age. How could that possibly be? His journey to hell had not gone well, his only replicators were Ron and me.

I got to my feet. It was though I was being assisted to rise as the control over my limbs did not appear to be of my own initiation. I moved towards the door and Dad, who was standing still, raised his arm. I turned, or I was turned, to stare towards my bed. I was still there, on the floor, but now lying on my side. I could see myself. I was through the door and in that cold bleak corridor, my speed increased to the point of anonymity. I was no-one. There was nothing to see as I had closed my eyes and simply let what was happening, happen!

Then awful reality came to bite me. I was in the séance room of Ellen in Windsor Place. Lamps were lit, and sitting there were Tom, Uncle Patrick, Jeremiah and Rose. Standing and talking to them was Ellen. On the table was a large pot. It was the pot I had seen in possession of the apparition of the monk in the Cathedral graveyard. I had never forgotten that vision. He was appealing to me to take it. I heard their conversation which brought me to anger. They were all in good spirits and extremely jovial.

Dad and I stood there. I felt a cold breeze move

over my face; it was a breeze that also affected my erstwhile friends. I watched how Rose pulled her coat up around her neck and Ellen went to check the doors but to no avail. The breeze was making Tom, and Jeremiah appear extremely uncomfortable. They were looking around at one another, and as the gale, from wherever it came, became intolerable, I looked at my father. His tortured being was now moving very slowly towards the table where the plundered pot was being held up against the wind by Ellen. Her mass of coal black hair streaked out behind, and I saw the terror in her face. The wind threw her away and lifted the pot smashing it on the ground. All present were lying on the floor; in fear of their lives. I was being pulled back towards the opposite end of the room and to the wall. The pot, in smashing, produced the brightest of lights. Out of the light a figure of a monk emerged, surely the monk I had seen in the graveyard. The terror that was gripping the living in that room was indicated by the harshness of their screams. Now it was their turn to feel the fear I had experienced many times before. The light burst into flame and the heat intense. The fire became an inferno. I was caught in the scorching wind which took me away from the room. I felt excruciating discomfort.

I flashed my eyes open. Stretching up at last, I felt the use of my limbs and attempted to get up. I was back in my cell. My writing was where I had left it. I started to scream incessantly which resulted in the door opening and three warders coming in. I was held and with great difficulty they put a restraining jacket over my body. I tried to explain to them about the fire in Windsor Place, but their patience was at a premium. They just would not listen. I was forced to lie on the floor and one of the men, who I knew well, and I thought was my friend, kicked me. His cries of 'shut up' made me realise that all the trust I collected over many months had disintegrated in just one night.

The door slammed shut and I was once again a lunatic in a cell. I ran to the door and shouted, 'Windsor Place is on fire. Help them. They're all going to die. Listen, please listen, they're all going to die'. There was no answer. Perhaps my lunacy had reached a new level and my destiny was to be incarcerated for life. The usual 'Shut up' felt heavy on my ears. The hurt in my head was deep.

## CHAPTER THIRTY-THREE

A most unusual day of the many I had suffered was about to dawn. It was two or three days after that awful experience in Windsor Place. A warder, who brought to my cell a platter of breakfast, came in. I expected ridicule, or even assault, but that did not happen. It was unusual to see just one warder in my cell, I am a big man and must be a handful to manage when angry. I was told to empty my sluice pot and then accompany the warders to an office. Someone wanted to see me. That is all I was told. My clothes were changed. The warders watched me intently as they appeared always aware of my madness and my unpredictability.

I was marched into the general visiting office and pushed down onto a chair. With a warder standing either side of me and one behind, I sat and stared at the world of the free, beyond a mesh booth. I waited around five minutes before I saw two men enter the space in front. One of them sat in a chair not one yard away. He was an impressive looking man, I would say in his fifties, wearing a smart suit, collar and tie. I will strive to write down the conversation as I remember it.

'I am Inspector Scott of the police detective department. What's your name? Do you know it?' I must have looked astonished at such a crass remark as he instantly spoke again. 'What is your name?'

'Elijah Llewellyn McNamara'.

'How old are you, Elijah?'

'What do you want to know for?' I was annoyed about the detective's brusque attitude; asylum people are not daft.

'You told warder Davies, that you were in a fire at Windsor Place and people had been killed. Is that right Mr Davies?' The detective looked towards the warder directly behind me.

'That is correct Sir', the warder replied.

'He named the people who died in a fire. Is that correct?'.

'Yes'. He was shouting out the names Tom, Rose, Ellen, Jeremiah and Patrick, if I remember correctly'.

'How did you know of this fire?' This question was put to me as the detective leant forward, his face almost touching the mesh. He repeated the question in a whisper with the words separated by long pauses. 'How did you know? Someone must have told you. Elijah, you knew even before we did. Was it one of your lunatic friends or one of their family that had done it? Tell me! Eli, how did you know?' His manner was officious in the extreme.

This man did not deserve respect. There was no compassion in his behaviour. I waited, then moved my head towards the mesh that divided us. I was about twelve inches from him. He also moved in close to me.

I said quite coldly with whispered words matching his, 'I was there'.

Detective Scott drew back and turned to his young associate who was sitting behind him.

'He was there, here that, he was there? He broke out of bedlam, done the murders and broke back in again'. They both laughed. I was angry, he had mentioned murders.

My question was heartfelt and needing of an empathetic reply, 'Ellen, Tom, Jeremiah, Uncle Patrick and Rose are definitely all dead?'

'We have what is left of them. Our enquiries discovered the names of the missing people that perished in this fire, except one. We have basic remains of five people. Who is this Patrick you were shouting about?'

For once his manner was amenable. I did not answer straight away, and his patience did not last long. He left his seat and shouted through the mesh. 'Who is Patrick?'

'My father's brother', I answered.

'So, the one person yet to be identified, you think is your Uncle Patrick do you?'

'Yes, Uncle Patrick McNamara'. He came over from Ireland some time ago for my father's funeral. He was in Windsor Place too. I saw him there'.

The reaction of the two detectives was to look at one another, there were no words. Scott told the other man to go and make telephone calls about my uncle.

'Elijah McNamara, you told warder Davies before

dawn on the morning of the fire, of trouble at Windsor Place and asked if your friends were safe. This was before we knew anything about the deaths there. Who told you about it? Come on, truth now'.

I looked at him and gently whispered the truth, 'I was there'.

He glared at me and snapped at one of the guards, 'Go and get warder Davies'. Turning to me he said, 'And you, stay there'.

He was agitated. I had no intention of going anywhere, even if I could. I was out of my room and beginning to comprehend what was going on. I knew, at that moment, that the visits of the spirits to me were fact. I knew that I was correct. Rose, Ellen, Tom, Patrick and Jeremiah were dead. A weight lifted off my shoulders, I believed that I would be released. Not a lunatic to be locked in an asylum, but an honest man. A proven honest man. The warder, Mr Davies, walked into the room, I saw the detective beckon him and both spoke in a confidential way.

Scott came back to face me. 'McNamara, who was it who told you about this fire?'

'No-one did. I was there'

'You were locked in your cell; you can't get out. You told warder Davies and he ignored it, until he read the newspaper. You knew before anyone else, so who told you?' His manner was aggressive; he was angry.

'I was there Mr Scott. The monk's pot exploded,

and I found myself back here'.

Scott laughed loudly and snapped 'The man's a fool. That's why you're here McNamara, a proven lunatic'. He turned to walk out but retraced his steps to say, 'Can you read McNamara?' I was insulted and did not answer. 'Then read the Holy book, learn what truth is'. His anger with me was profound and I with him.

He thanked the warders. I was pulled to my feet and marched off down the corridor to my room. Pushing me in, the door closed. The hatch opened and the friendliest of the two warders peered through.

'Well Eli, plenty to write about today. When you see your Dad again, give him our regards? I heard laughter in the corridor. 'I best throw away the key. You ain't coming out of here now boy'. Then with a final flourish, he shouted, 'Ever!'

His fellow pulled him away from the hatch. He grinned and said very deliberately, 'The madding of Eli McNamara'. The title of my manuscript had been noted and the information passed around among the staff here. He then said it again, then once more. He was taunting me, laughing at me. Before he got more words out, I ran at the door. It was too late to slam the hatch.

I pushed my arms through and screamed, 'Dad, Dad, tell them. Dad'

'Shut up McNamara! You'll give the madhouse a bad name'. He laughed, pushed my arm back in, slammed the hatch and was gone.

The walls were closing in on me and I could not take it anymore. My screams turned to howls before I collapsed on my mattress crying, like a boy after a whipping. I heard the shouts of the warders telling me to shut up my noise. I had lost everyone I ever cherished in my life. My mother and siblings were the only ones left who could give me love and they had gone. Where they were I did not know, as they did not want to know me. My howls did not go unnoticed by the others, all were howling back from their little desolate worlds. I have no-one to speak for me, all dead. My mother may as well be too. And here I am. I had no more visits, no detectives, no mother or siblings, no-one to ask about anything. The magistrate who I parade in front of every few months in the asylum hall, always nods and says the same words, 'He looks alright to me. Next'. I am taken back to my room as another is marched in.

As the years have passed, my once handsome appearance has crumbled. My long, vermin dotted hair is cut every three months, the barber who visits the cell is protected by guards. He always says, 'Name?'

I tell him, he writes it down on a pad, scissors my hair and beard, then exits. No other words are spoken. There is one evidential path I long to walk. The path to the marker I pushed deeply into the earth, the marker to more than treasure, the marker to freedom.

Believe me reader of this truth. The greed of the living is nothing compared to the greed of the dead. Signed: Elijah L McNamara. Bedlam. 1929.  **END**

*The Royal (Tudor) Public House is demolished.*
*The Red Lion Public House is long demolished.*
*The Globe Hotel still stands.*
*Scott Street is demolished.*
*The Cottage public house (the Roath Cottage) has closed.*
*The brewery has gone. The location is now a food and drink quarter.*
*Llandaff Cathedral can be visited.*
*Castell Coch or Castell Morgraig, may be the wooded locations of the alleged buried hoard.*
*The cemetery (Cathays) is one of the largest in the United Kingdom, and populated with graveyard voices, just waiting for their stories to be told.*

**JOHN F WAKE BOOKS BY WORDCATCHER PUBLISHING**

*The Cruel Streets Revisited.*
*Cardiff. Those Cruel and Savage Streets.*
*Why Shoot David Thomas?*
*Horrors of the Dead House.*
*Darkest Cardiff.*
*The Mermaid of Cardigan Bay.*
*Cardiff City Police. The Final Years.*
*The Goose Maiden (Drama)*

**BY PWNTAN PUBLISHING**

*The Newtown Riot, Cardiff 1859. (Case file)*
*Cardiff – Crime and Injustice*

PWNTAN

Printed in Great Britain
by Amazon